# "You said that it would be difficult to be alone together at the Villa Fortuna..."

Lorenzo nodded, resigned. "The moment my sister, Isabella, learns I have guests, she will come rushing to meet you."

Jess bit her lip. "Won't she find it odd? That you've invited me to stay at your house?"

Lorenzo sat in silence for some time, his eyes fixed on their entwined hands. "She will be very surprised," he said at last, his voice deeper and more uneven than it had been. "Because I have never invited a woman there before." He looked up again, his eyes alight with an urgency that took her breath away. "I did not mean to say this. At least, not tonight. I told myself I must wait, be patient. But, *Dio*, I have wasted enough of my life already." His grasp tightened. "I knew from the first moment I saw you that I wanted you for my own. Not for a *relazione*—a love affair, but forever. I want you for my wife, Jessamy."

# The Dysarts

*A family with a passion for life—and for love.*

Welcome to the second book in **The Dysarts**, a wonderful new series by bestselling author Catherine George. *Lorenzo's Reward* tells the story of the second Dysart Sister, Jess, whose experiences have led her to believe that she will never enjoy intimacy with a man—until she finds herself pursued by darkly handsome Italian Lorenzo Forli. Is Lorenzo sincere when he talks about claiming Jess as his wife? Or will it be reward enough for him to seduce her into his bed?

Over the coming months, you'll get to know each member of the Dysart family, and share in their trials and joys, their hopes and dreams, as they live their lives with passion—and for love.

Look out in November for a special short story by Catherine George—when the Dysarts celebrate Christmas, and the arrival of a new baby. Available in the *Mistletoe Miracles* story collection. ISBN 0-373-83475-6

Coming next year:
Adam's story

# Catherine George

## LORENZO'S REWARD

The Dysarts

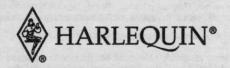

# HARLEQUIN®

TORONTO • NEW YORK • LONDON
AMSTERDAM • PARIS • SYDNEY • HAMBURG
STOCKHOLM • ATHENS • TOKYO • MILAN • MADRID
PRAGUE • WARSAW • BUDAPEST • AUCKLAND

ISBN 0-373-12203-9

LORENZO'S REWARD

First North American Publication 2001.

This edition published by arrangement with Harlequin Books S.A.

® and TM are trademarks of the publisher. Trademarks indicated with ® are registered in the United States Patent and Trademark Office, the Canadian Trade Marks Office and in other countries.

Visit us at www.eHarlequin.com

**Printed in U.S.A.**

# CHAPTER ONE

THE crowded pub was hot, smoke-filled, and full of men in suits talking business over lunch. Jess eyed her watch impatiently, willing Simon to hurry, then looked up to find a complete stranger watching her intently from the far end of the bar. Jess felt an odd plummeting sensation in the pit of her stomach when dark, heavy-lidded eyes lit with incredulous recognition as they met hers. She glanced over her shoulder, sure he must be looking at some other woman, but there was no other female in sight.

Jess looked back again, which was a mistake. This time she couldn't look away. Heat rose in her face. Irritably she ordered herself to stop sitting there like a hypnotised rabbit, her pulse suddenly erratic as the man put down his drink and with purpose began to push his way through the crowd towards her. But before he could reach her two other men joined him, barring his way. The stranger shrugged expressively, signalling regret, and Jess finally broke eye contact. Then it dawned on her that one of his companions was Mr Jeremy Lonsdale, unrecognisable for a moment minus his barristers wig and gown. But when the third member of the trio turned his head she gasped in utter consternation. He was all too familiar, with eyes which blazed in incredulous affront when Jess panicked at the sight of him, spun around and fled from the pub, with Simon Hollister, her astonished lunch companion, in hot pursuit.

Jess dodged through honking traffic, and ran like a deer

up the road to the courthouse, to subject herself to the
usual security process inside. She was still gasping for
breath when Simon caught up with her in the jury restaurant.

"What the hell was all that about?" he panted.

"Prosecuting—Counsel—was there. With chums."
Jess heaved in a lungful of air. "One of them was
Roberto Forli, my sister's ex-boyfriend," she finished in
a rush.

Simon whistled. "And we jurors are forbidden con-
nection to anyone at all on the case."

"Exactly!"

"How well do you know the man?"

"I've only met him once."

"Did Lonsdale see you?"

"I don't think so. He had his back to me."

Simon smiled reassuringly. "Then it's probably all
right. Anyway, we'll soon know if your friend grassed
on you. Let's grab something to eat before we're called.
I left our lunch on the bar when you took off."

But after her mad dash in the midday heat Jess couldn't
face the thought of food. Her mind was too full of the
unexpected meeting with Roberto Forli. And with the
stranger in his company. The memory of those dark, intent eyes sent shivers down her spine. The man had obviously recognised her from somewhere. But where? And
when? Jess forced herself back to the present with an
effort, and gulped down the rest of her mineral water as
the jury was called back into the court.

As she took her seat in the jury box Jess buttoned her
jacket against the cold of the courtroom, which was arctic
compared with the summer day outside. According to bus
driver Phil, the comedian in their group, the courtroom
was kept cool to keep the jury awake during the longer

discourses, and at the same time prevent heatstroke for the judge and barristers in their archaic horsehair wigs and black gowns.

While they waited for the judge Jess firmly blanked the lunchtime incident from her mind by thinking back over her two weeks of jury service. She was glad, now, of the experience, but the first day had been daunting. After waiting in line to pass through an airport-style metal detector she had been directed to the jury restaurant, an airport-style cafeteria packed with people queuing for coffee, reading newspapers, or just sitting staring into space if they'd managed to find a chair. Later, in an empty courtroom with the other newcomers, she had watched a video which set out the rules, but a wait of two days had elapsed before she was called into service.

The clerk of the court had shuffled cards and read out names as usual, but this time Jessamy Dysart was among the chosen. She had been led off to a courtroom, and with eleven of her peers sworn in as a member of the jury. At first glance the dark wood and leather of the courtroom, though impressive enough, had seemed a lot smaller than on television. Jess had been rather disconcerted to find herself at such close quarters not only with the prisoner in the dock, but with the barristers and solicitors facing the judge in the well of the court.

Now there was only another day of a different trial to go, with a different batch of jurors. This time Jess was seated in the front of the jury box next to Simon Hollister. He had made a beeline for her from the first day, and frankly admitted that his original intention had been to avoid jury duty by pleading pressure of work in his marketing job in the City. But once actually there in the courthouse an unexpected sense of civic duty had made him stay.

"Added to the prospect of a fortnight coming into close contact with you, Jess," he'd added, with a grin.

Jess had taken this with a pinch of salt. Simon was a charmer, and she liked him, but she also liked Edward, the ex-headmaster, and June, the office cleaner, and most of her fellow jurors. However, she longed for this particular trial to be over. The young woman in the dock, Prosecuting Counsel alleged, had knowingly smuggled drugs into the country in her luggage. Like Jess she was in her mid-twenties, but with eyes dark-ringed in a pale, strained face, and from the evidence there seemed little doubt that she was guilty.

Previously Jess had preferred to eat a sandwich lunch in the jury restaurant with the others. But today she had given in to Simon's coaxing, glad to escape from the memory of the defendant's hopeless eyes. Now Jess wished she'd stayed put as usual. The fascinating stranger's interest had intrigued her, and in other circumstances she would have liked to meet him. But not when he came as one of a package with Roberto Forli and Prosecuting Counsel.

Jess waited in trepidation as the afternoon session began, fully expecting the judge to stop the proceedings. But to her vast relief everything went on as usual, and instead of pointing a dramatic finger at her Mr Jeremy Lonsdale merely got to his feet to make his closing speech for the prosecution. When the barrister sat down at last Simon gave a discreet thumbs-up sign. Afterwards Defence Counsel's speech proved to be mainly a criticism of Prosecution's case, with interminable reminders to the jury about burden of proof and miscarriages of justice. Long before he finished Jess bitterly regretted the reckless volume of water downed before coming into court. Hot with embarrassment, she was forced to raise a hand at last when the barrister paused for breath. With the judge's permission the usher escorted all members of the jury from the box to lock them in the jury room where eleven of them waited while Jess, crimson-faced, retired to their private cloakroom. Afterwards they all filed back into the court again to hear Defence Counsel come to a conclusion. When he achieved this at long last the judge ruled that it was time to finish for the day. He would leave his summing up for the morning.

"Not to worry, love," whispered June afterwards. "Don't be embarrassed. Nature calls everyone—even the judge."

The June sunshine was warm as Jess drove home through rush hour. Moving from one set of traffic lights to the next in slow progression, she was so preoccupied with the thoughts of the fascinating stranger she almost shot a red light at one point, and glued her attention to the traffic afterwards instead. The hot, crowded city streets filled Jess with sudden longing for Friars Wood, the cool house perched on the cliffs overlooking the Wye Valley, and the meal her mother would be concocting for the family at that very moment. Just one more day to go, she consoled herself, then she could go home for a break.

Jess managed to park near her flat in Bayswater, then trudged along the terrace of tall white houses, glad to get back to a home far more peaceful these days, since Fiona Todd had moved out to live with her man. Jess and her remaining flatmate, Emily Shaw, were now the only tenants, an arrangement which worked very amicably.

When Jess got in Emily was lying on the sofa, watching television. "Hi," she said, turning the set off. "My word, you look done in. What's up?"

Jess groaned. "Have I had a fraught day!"

"Is it desperately hush-hush, or are you allowed to tell me?"

"This bit I can! I ran into Roberto Forli in a pub at lunchtime."

Emily's big eyes widened. "*Really?* Your sister's ex from Florence? What's he doing here in London?"

"No idea. Whatever it was I wish he'd been doing it somewhere else," said Jess irritably.

"Why?" said Emily, astonished.

"It's a long story."

"But jolly interesting, by the sound of it."

Jess took a deep breath. "Simon Hollister, the marketing bloke on the jury with me, asked me out for a swift lunch. By sheer bad luck we hit on the same pub as Prosecuting Counsel."

"No!"

Jess described the incident with Roberto Forli to her riveted friend. But, for reasons she wasn't quite sure of, made no mention of the stranger. "We're forbidden contact with anyone connected to the court, of course, so when I saw Roberto all chummy with Prosecuting Counsel I shot out of the pub like greased lightning and did a runner back to the courthouse."

"Did Roberto see you?"

"You bet he did." Jess collapsed into a chair, grateful for the fruit juice her friend handed over. "Wonderful. I needed this. Thank goodness you were home early today."

Emily Shaw worked for an executive in a credit card company, and it was rare that she was home at this hour. "Mr Boss Man's away, and I've been slaving like mad to get everything shipshape before I take off on my hols. I developed a nasty little headache after lunch, so I knocked off early for once."

"I should think so." Jess eyed her closely. "You look horribly peaky. Have you taken any painkillers?"

"Yes, Nurse. And I'm going to bed early." Emily grinned. "You should do the same for once."

"I probably will." Jess smiled ruefully. "Pity I had to offend Roberto like that. You should have seen his face when I bolted!"

"Well, don't keep me in suspense—what happened when you went back into the jury box? Did the judge excommunicate you, or whatever?"

"No, thank goodness. But while Defence Counsel was droning on I realised I shouldn't have drunk so much water." Jess giggled as she described the trooping out of the entire jury on her account. "There's only one loo in the jury room, and it's not exactly soundproof. I think I'm still blushing."

"Oh, bad luck!" Emily laughed, then eyed Jess speculatively. "I wonder why Leonie's ex is in London?"

"No idea." Jess sighed. "Pity he was with Prosecuting Counsel. In any other circumstances I'd have enjoyed a chat with him very much." And, more to the point, achieved an introduction to the interesting stranger at the same time.

"Never mind," consoled Emily. "Perhaps Leo will know when you go home for the wedding."

Jess brightened. "Which now seems plain sailing, thank goodness. I was getting a bit tense about the way things were dragging on, in case I had to dash straight back after the wedding to go to court on Monday, but with a bit of luck the case will finish tomorrow. Lucky for me, anyway," she added, sobering.

"Cheer up—the weekend forecast looks good." Emily grinned. "The sun is sure to shine for Leonie on Sunday, anyway. The minute I set foot in a plane to fly away from it Britain always swelters in a heatwave.''

"Since you're off to sunny Italy it doesn't matter." Jess sighed. "I wish I was going with you. After seven years apart Jonah and Leo were all for dashing off to a register office right away, of course, but when they were persuaded to wait for a conventional June wedding I hadn't the heart to say the date clashed with my holiday."

"You know nothing would have kept you from Leonie's wedding! Not to worry; we'll do a holiday together some other time. And *my* sister was in raptures when I suggested she stepped into the breach."

"Who's looking after the children?"

"My mother's taking turns with the other grandma. And Jack gets home to supervise bathtime and bed, anyway. I told Celia to relax—they'll all cope."

"Of course they will. And I'll use the time off to laze about at home." Jess yawned widely. "I'm off for a bath."


Jess was towelling thick layers of flaxen hair when Emily banged on the bathroom door.

"Phone call for you," she called. "Guess who?"

"Surprise me."

"A sexy-sounding gent by the name of Forli!"

"*What*? Tell me you're pulling my leg, Em!" said Jess, throwing open the door in dismay.

"Of course I'm not," said Emily indignantly. "He's hanging on as we speak, dearie, so get yourself to the phone."

Jess shook her head violently. "I still can't talk to him."

"What on earth shall I say?"

"Tell him I'm in the bath. Asleep. Anything. Why didn't you say I was out?"

"I didn't realise a phone call was taboo as well." Emily shook her head. "Honestly, Jess, any woman in her right mind would *kill* to listen to that voice purring down the line. Who would know?" She flung up her hands. "All right, all right. I'll lie through my teeth and swear you're prostrate with a migraine."

"Perfect. If I'm not I should be!"

When Jess joined Emily minutes later her friend grinned as she ladled cream and smoked salmon over bowls of steaming pasta.

"I'm afraid the gentleman didn't believe a word of it. But he was much too civilised to blame the messenger."

"Damn, damn, damn!" said Jess bitterly. "Any other time I'd have been delighted to talk to him."

"I believe you. Is he tall, dark and handsome to match the voice?"

"Not quite." That particular description belonged to the third man in the equation. "Roberto's tall enough, but fairish in that olive-skinned, Latin sort of way. A bit of a star on the ski-slopes, according to Leo."

"Smouldering blue eyes, of course," said Emily, smacking her lips.

"What *have* you been reading lately? Actually his eyes are dark like mine."

"Smouldering *black* eyes, then. Even better."

Jess's heart gave a sudden lurch at the memory of dark eyes which had smouldered so effectively she couldn't get them out of her mind. She ground her teeth in frustration. If only she'd been able to talk to Roberto he could have introduced her. Why did this kind of thing never go right for her? She eyed Emily hopefully. "I don't suppose Roberto gave you his number? I could happily ring him tomorrow, *after* the trial.''

"Sorry. A second rebuff must have been too much for the poor guy.''

"I'll bet. Especially as it's not long since my sister jilted him. We Dysart girls really know how to treat a man, don't we?'' Jess ate her favourite supper with less relish than it deserved. "Maybe Leo knows his number. If so I'll ring to apologise.'' And casually ask who the friend might be.

"Don't just apologise—grovel!'' advised Emily.

"You haven't even met the man.''

"I don't have to! Just listening to that voice was enough.''

Next day the proceedings in court were over sooner than expected. The judge reminded the jury of the exact meaning of the indictment, of what the Prosecution was obliged to prove to win its case and what the Defence must have done to persuade the jury to acquit, and concluded by telling the jury it was entirely up to them to decide. The ushers took an oath to keep the jury in a private and convenient place, and Jess and her fellow jurors were led off to the jury room and locked in to make their deliberations.

This time the facts were so conclusive that the jury members were reluctantly unanimous, and back in court later Edward, their foreman, delivered the verdict of guilty. Up to that point Jess had been very sorry for the young woman in the dock, but to her surprise Prosecuting Counsel justified the jury's verdict by disclosing a prior conviction of a similar nature before the judge passed sentence.

Afterwards the twelve jury members went off to the

pub Jess had raced from the day before. But this time there was no sign of Roberto Forli and Jeremy Lonsdale, nor, most disappointing of all, of the third member of the trio.

"Let's keep in touch, Jess," said Simon Hollister, as they emerged with the others into hot afternoon sunlight. "If I give you a ring soon, will you have dinner with me?"

"I'd love to," agreed Jess. "Not yet awhile, though. I'm off home to Gloucestershire for my sister's wedding tomorrow, and I'm staying on for a few days."

"Lucky old you," he said enviously. "I'm back to the City grind on Monday. I'll ring you in a week or so, then."

Jess nodded, then beckoned to June. "Time I went. I'm giving our friend a lift. See you, Simon."

The moment she got back to the flat Jess rang home. "Hi, Mother, it's me. The trial finished today after all, so I can stay on after the wedding with a light heart."

"Thank heavens for that," said Frances Dysart with relief. "How are you, darling? Tired?"

"Exhausted. How are things there? Mad panic on all sides?"

"Not a bit of it. The bride is floating about on a pink cloud and Fenny, needless to say, is bursting with excitement. But Kate's a bit tense. She's only halfway through her exams."

"I can't believe she's worried about failing! Kate's the brains of the family." Jess chuckled ruefully. "Leo got the looks and Adam the charm, whereas poor old me—"

"Whereas poor old you," echoed her mother dryly, "are the sexiest, according to your brother."

Jess was astounded. "*Really?* When did Adam say that?"

"This morning. He arrived with a carload of laundry—in time for lunch, of course."

Jess laughed. "How did his Finals go?"

"He refuses to commit himself. He's going back to Edinburgh to paint it red after the wedding, but for now I think he's just relieved the exams are over."

"I bet he is. And how about you and Dad? Are you worn out with all the excitement?"

"Not in the least. Everything's under control. What time are you arriving tomorrow?"

"I'll ring when I start off. Jury work's more tiring than I expected—I really need a lie-in tomorrow before I have my hair cut. I should be with you some time in the afternoon. And mind you take it easy, Mother, don't work too hard. See you tomorrow. Can you float the bride towards the phone now?"

Leonie Dysart greeted her sister with such exuberance Jess felt wistful, wondering how it felt to be so much in love. And to know with such certainty that her feelings were returned.

"Sorry, Leo, what did you say?" she said quickly.

"I asked how you were feeling after your stint in court."

"A bit tired, as we speak, but don't worry. I'll be firing on all cylinders on the day." Jess paused. "Leo, this is a bit of a long shot, but I don't suppose you'd know how to contact Roberto Forli? Here in this country, I mean? You'll never believe this, but I bumped into him yesterday—"

"Don't I know it! What on earth was all that about? He rang here afterwards and told me you took one look at him in a pub somewhere and ran for your life. He sounded so stroppy I was surprised when he asked for your telephone number. Did he get in touch last night?"

"Yes, he did. But I couldn't speak to him then, either."

"Why not?" demanded her sister in astonishment. "I thought you liked him."

"I *do*." Jess heaved a sigh, then explained the problem in detail.

"Oh, Jess, what bad luck! I knew Roberto had a barrister friend he sometimes stays with in London."

"Unfortunately the friend was Prosecuting Counsel on the case I was sitting in on. So I thought if I could ring him to explain—"

"You don't have to," said Leonie, sounding rather odd. "You'll see him on Sunday. I've invited him to the wedding."

"What? And he's actually *coming*?" said Jess, astonished. "How does Jonah feel about that? Doesn't he mind having his wedding cluttered up with your former lovers?"

"Just one," said Leonie tartly. "Not that Roberto was ever my lover, as you well know. Anyway, I invited the Ravellos, who own the school in Florence. And since it's through them that I met Roberto when I was teaching there it seemed only polite to send him an invitation, too. Mind you, I never dreamed he'd accept."

"Jonah's not put out?"

"He's all for it."

Jess chuckled. "You mean he's very happy for Roberto to look on, grinding his teeth, while you take Jonah Savage for your lawful wedded husband."

"Exactly." Leonie gave a wry little laugh. "Anyway, Jess, do try to smooth things over with Roberto. He's a good friend of mine, remember, and I'm fond of him. Poor man. Women invariably chase after Roberto Forli, not run away from him."

# CHAPTER TWO

THE DRIVE home was long and hot, the motorway crowded with holiday traffic, and Jess felt her spirits lift when she saw the twin towers of the older Severn bridge soaring white against the blue sky. She hummed happily in tune with the car radio as she drove across the bridge, then down through Chepstow and on for the remaining miles towards home. She swept in through the gates of Friars Wood at last, gunned the car up the bends of the drive past the Stables where Adam lived, and roared past the main house to park in a crunch of gravel in her usual spot under the trees near the summerhouse at the end of the terrace.

Jess sounded her horn, indignant when no one came rushing out of the house to greet her. Then she jumped out of the car, laughing, as six-year-old Fenella came hurtling up the garden, with a large golden retriever in panting pursuit. Leonie came following behind in more leisurely fashion, attired in shrunken vest top, khaki shorts and battered old sneakers, her bronze hair bundled up in an untidy knot.

"You're a very messy bride, Leo!" called Jess, hugging Fenny as she fended off Marzi, who was frisking around them in a frenzy of excitement. "Where is everyone?"

"Adam's driven Kate to her friend's house to get some books," panted Fenny, gazing, round-eyed, at Jess's hair.

"And Dad's taken Mother to the hairdresser," said Leonie. "Fenny got impatient, waiting for you, so we went off to throw a ball for the dog before he's banished to the farm for the weekend.'' She gave Jess a kiss, then stood back, grinning. "I love the hair.''

"Do you? Really?'' Jess smiled, relieved. "I suppose I should have asked your approval first. It's your wedding. But I was tired of my girly bob. I fancied something wilder for a change.''

"Dad will hate it,'' said Leonie, laughing. "But I love the way it falls over one eye like that. Dead sexy. Come and have tea; you must be hot after the drive. Fen, shall I take Marzi's lead?''

"No, I can do it,'' insisted the little girl.

"You're obviously not bothering with a hairdresser, Leo,'' commented Jess, as they went into the cool house together.

"Nope. I'll wash the flowing locks myself, as usual. I just want to look my normal self.''

"Which is exactly what Jonah requires, of course. Always has,'' added Jess.

Leonie nodded, her dark eyes luminous. "I know. I'm so lucky.''

"So is Jonah,'' said Jess gruffly. "Now, where's that tea?''

"Mother said you'd probably skip lunch,'' said Leonie. "So I made you some salad, and hid some of Mother's little mushroom tarts from Adam.''

"And the coconut cake,'' said Fenny, eyes gleaming as they fastened on the snowy confection under a glass dome. "Can I have some, Leo? Please?''

"So what's happening tonight?'' said Jess, helping herself to salad.

"Jonah's having dinner with his family in Pennington tonight, at the company flat, and we'll just have a family supper here.'' Leonie cut a slice of cake for Fenny.

"Roberto's staying in Pennington too, with the Ravellos," she said casually. "So you could ring the Chesterton tonight and have a chat with him. If you like."

Jess choked on a crumb of pastry, her dark eyes bright with dismay as they met her sister's. "Must I?"

"I thought you might like to. So that everything's nice and friendly for tomorrow."

Jess's groan was cut off by the arrival of Tom and Frances Dysart, who came hurrying in with Adam and Kate close behind them. Jess sprang up to embrace them all, and there was general laughter when her father blenched theatrically as he noticed her hair. The kitchen filled with exuberant noise as all the Dysarts began talking at once and the dog began barking in excitement in counterpoint. Jess breathed in a deep, happy sigh. She was home.

After supper, which they ate early so that Fenny could share it with them, Adam went for a run down to the farm to hand over the dog, Kate took herself off to revise for her next exam, and Frances and Tom Dysart retired to the study for some peace and quiet while Jess admired wedding presents in Leonie's room.

"I hope Jonah won't be disappointed because I'm not wearing a meringue-type wedding dress and veil and so on," said Leonie, as she repacked a Baccarat crystal vase.

"Of course he won't!" said Jess with scorn. "The dress is perfect. What did you decide on for your hair in the end?"

"I wasn't going to wear anything at first. But when Dad mentioned a jewellery auction he was holding at Dysart's, Jonah bid for the most amazing pair of antique earrings for a wedding present—showers of baroque pearls on tiny gold chains, with a matching brooch. I've

sewn the brooch to a silk barrette to fasten in my hair.''
Leonie took it from its nest of tissue paper and secured
a tress of bronze hair back with it. ''What do you think?''

Jess eyed the result with approval. ''Perfect! Now put
the earrings on so I can see the full effect.''

Leonie rummaged in a drawer, then spun round, her
eyes meeting her sister's in sudden panic. ''Jess, they're
not here—Jonah took them into a jeweller in Pennington
to rethread some of the pearls. And it's Saturday night!
What if he's forgotten to collect them?'' Sudden tears
poured down her face, astonishing her sister. ''I wanted
everything to be so *perfect*—''

''Hey, hey,'' said Jess, dismayed.

''Don't get upset. Ring him now and ask him.''

''I'm not supposed to,'' sobbed Leonie. ''It's unlucky
the night before the wedding!''

''Then I will.'' Jess passed her sister a bunch of tissues. ''Calm down, Leo. This isn't like you!''

''Sorry.'' Leonie blew her nose, then gave Jess a wa-
tery, radiant smile. ''It must be hormones. Can you keep
a secret? I haven't told Mother, in case she's worried
about me tomorrow, in fact I haven't told a soul yet—
not even Jonah—but I found out today for sure that I'm
pregnant.''

Jess enveloped her sister in a crushing hug. ''And
you're thrilled to bits, obviously. Wonderful! When are
you going to give Jonah the glad news?''

Leonie gave a wicked grin. ''I thought tomorrow night,
maybe? *Late* tomorrow night, in the honeymoon suite in
our hotel in Paris. A sort of extra wedding present.''

Jess chuckled, then reached for her sister's cellphone.
''Right, then. Let's ring the bridegroom. You want ear-
rings, little mother, you shall have earrings—even if
Jonah has to bribe the jeweller to open up again tonight.''

But when Jonah was questioned it seemed he'd collected them the day before and merely forgotten to hand them over. Jess gave him a laughing telling-off, and, when he was all for driving over right away, informed him that Leonie forbade him to set foot in the vicinity of Friars Wood that night.

"You stay put. I'll come and collect them." She made a face at Leonie. "But the Chesterton's a lot nearer for me than your flat, Jonah, so be a love and save me a trip right across town on a Saturday night. Meet me in the bar there to hand them over? Right. Yes, I'll tell her. She's blowing a kiss as we speak. See you in half an hour or so."

"You're going to kill two birds with one stone?" said Leonie, eyes sparkling.

Jess sighed, resigned. "I suppose so. Anything to make your day perfect. So I'll fetch the earrings and make my peace with your ex-lover at the same time, and if ever I get married I'll think of something *really* difficult you can do for me in exchange."

"Anything," said Leonie fervently.

"I'll hold you to that. Jonah sent his love, of course." Jess glanced down at her halter top and ivory linen trousers. "If I just wear the jacket belonging to these will I do?"

"Slap some more make-up on and take those stilt-heeled strappy things to change into when you get there." Leonie grinned and kissed her fingertips. "Before he met me Roberto was very partial to sexy blondes. He'll melt at the sight of you."

And in doing so impart some information about his companion at the pub, maybe. Unknown to Leonie, Jess had secretly jumped at the chance to go out. She felt oddly restless. Wedding fever, she decided, as she neared the outskirts of the town. Until recently a committed relationship of any kind had held little attraction for her, except as something far off in the future. But since Leonie and Jonah's reunion a gradual feeling of discontent had crept up on her, a hankering after something different from the no-strings, light-hearted arrangements she'd preferred up to now. But the fleeting encounter with the dark stranger had jolted her into a sudden longing for the kind of relationship Leo had with Jonah Savage. Not that she was likely to achieve that in the foreseeable future, Jess thought irritably as she picked her way across the gravel of the Chesterton car park.

Relieved to find that Roberto Forli was nowhere in sight for the moment, Jess made for the bar, and spotted the tall figure of Jonah Savage talking to the barman.

"Jess," exclaimed Jonah, smiling, his green eyes alight with welcome as he came forward to give her a hug. "Sexy haircut!"

"Hi, Jonah. Glad you approve."

"You look positively edible. Shame I'm promised to Another," he teased. "What can I get you?"

"Just some fruit juice, then I must go straight back."

Jonah gave the order, then leaned close to Jess with a probing look. "So tell me. How is she?"

"Leo's fine. A bit emotional when she remembered the earrings, but otherwise in perfectly good nick, I promise you." Jess nursed her sister's secret with hidden glee as she sipped her orange juice. "How's the groom?"

"Nervous as hell. God knows why," he added, "marrying Leo is all I've ever wanted since the day I met her."

"I know." Jess drained the glass, feeling edgy, for once wanting Jonah to make himself scarce so she could find Roberto and get her apologies over and done with. "Thanks, Jonah. Must dash."

He looked surprised. "Why the rush? My parents hoped you'd come to the flat for a drink. My aunt's with them."

"Sorry, I must get back to Leo. The earrings were a vital necessity before the bride could go happy to bed. Give the three of them my love."

"Jess," said Jonah, frowning. "Are you being straight with me? You'd tell me if something was wrong?"

She laughed indulgently, and reached up to pat his cheek. "Scout's honour, the blushing bride can't wait to sprint down the aisle to you. But we all want an early night tonight. Ditto for you, too—you can stay up late tomorrow."

Jonah grinned. "I seriously doubt that."

"Spare my blushes, please!" she retorted, fluttering her eyelashes.

"Jess, I really appreciate your coming all this way for Leo's sake," said Jonah as they left the bar. "Drive carefully."

"I will." She returned his affectionate hug and kiss with warmth, took the box he gave her, and stowed it carefully in her bag. "Must make a pitstop before I go back. Don't wait. See you tomorrow, brother-in-law."

Jess waved Jonah off, then hurried off to the cloakroom, needing to make a few repairs as self-defence before she went in search of Roberto Forli. But no search was necessary. When she returned to the foyer, lips retouched and hair in place, he was waiting for her. And he had company. Jess's heart gave a great lurch, missed a couple of beats, then resumed with a force which made her feel giddy. She felt hollow, hardly able to breathe,

the blood pounding through her veins at a dizzying rate as she recognised Roberto's companion.

Like Roberto, he wore a pale linen suit, but his hair was thick and dark, and the unforgettable black eyes held hers with the look Jess had persuaded herself she'd imagined. A faint smile played at the corners of his mouth while she gazed at him mutely, for the first time in her life struck completely dumb.

"Will you not introduce us, Roberto?" said the stranger at last, his voice deep-toned and husky, with a hint of accent which accelerated Jess's pulse to an alarming degree.

"I will do so at once, before she runs away again." Roberto, who had been looking from one to the other with narrowed eyes, bowed formally. "Miss Jessamy Dysart, allow me to present my brother, Lorenzo Forli."

Jess murmured an incoherent greeting, and Lorenzi Forli took her hand and raised it to his lips. Jess disengaged her hand swiftly, and forced her attention back to Roberto. She had met him only once before, when she'd played an unwanted third at dinner in this very hotel the night Leonie had informed Roberto Forli she was marrying another man. Then, they had spent a pleasant hour together after Jonah had arrived to take Leonie home, and Roberto, despite the circumstances, had been charm itself to Jess. Tonight, however, his manner was hostile. Nor did Jess blame him for it.

"I'm glad to see you again, Roberto." She held out her hand to him. "How are you?"

He took the hand and bowed, unsmiling. "I am well. And you?"

His chill courtesy made it difficult to embark on the apology she was very conscious that he deserved. "I'm fine. I came on an errand for Leo. My sister," she explained, turning to Lorenzo.

"I am acquainted with the beautiful Leonie," he informed her. And Leo had never thought fit to *mention* him?

"How is the bride?" asked Roberto. "Radiant and beautiful as always?"

"Even more so at the moment," Jess informed him.

Roberto's eyes flickered for an instant. "Ah, yes. You know I am invited to the wedding?"

"Leo told me. But I was surprised you'd want to come," she said frankly.

Roberto shrugged his shoulders in the way Jess remembered well from their first meeting. "I was coming to your country at this time for other reasons."

"Is it a business trip?" asked Jess. "I've forgotten what you actually do, I'm afraid."

"We are involved in hotels," said Lorenzo, moving closer. "Miss Dysart, please drink a glass of wine with us."

"I'm sorry, I can't," said Jess with deep regret. "I'm driving, I must get back."

"We saw you with Leonie's *fidanzato*." Roberto informed her, his eyes bright with unexpected malice. "But he left before we could congratulate him."

"I came to collect some earrings from Jonah," said Jess. "Leo's wearing them tomorrow, and he'd forgotten to hand them over."

"Neither your brother nor your father could do this?"

Jess stiffened at his tone. "They wanted to," she said shortly. "But I had my reasons for coming myself."

"Of course you did," said Roberto with open sarcasm.

"Enough, Roberto," commanded Lorenzo. "Rejoin the Ravellos. I will escort Miss Dysart to her car."

Roberto, obviously about to protest, received a quelling look from his brother, and reluctantly acquiesced. He nodded coldly to Jess. "Please give my—my regards to Leonie. *Arrivederci*!" And before she could embark on her apology he strode off.

"There's something I must explain to Roberto," began Jess in a rush, and would have gone after him, but Lorenzo Forli took her arm.

"Leave him."

"But he's obviously put out with me—I need to apologise for running away that day in London," she said, ignoring the fact that Lorenzo Forli's touch seemed to be scorching through her sleeve.

"Roberto is 'put out' as you say, not only because you ran away at the sight of him, but because he believes that you are in love with Leonie's *fidanzato*," he informed her, as he escorted her outside to the car park.

"*What?*" Jess stared up at him in disbelief.

Lorenzo shrugged. "He is sure that you came here tonight for a few stolen moments before your sister's lover lost you tomorrow."

Jess stopped dead, and wrenched her arm away, her eyes blazing as she glared up into the dark, imperious face. "That's nonsense," she snapped.

"Is it?" he demanded.

"Of course it is!" Jess looked him in the eye. "Look, Signor Forli, I came here tonight purely to please my sister, and to explain to Roberto why it was impossible to speak to him on Thursday—"

"All of which may be true. But I think Roberto can be forgiven for his mistake." Lorenzo Forli's eyes locked with hers. "I also saw you embrace your sister's lover," he informed her.

"So did several other people," she retorted, incensed.

"There was nothing furtive about it. I find Roberto's insinuations deeply offensive. Yours, too, Goodnight, Signor Forli." Jess stormed off blindly towards the car, in such a tearing hurry she caught one tall, slender heel in a patch of loose gravel and fell heavily on her hands and knees.

Lorenzo raced to pull her to her feet. "*Dio*—are you hurt?"

"Only my dignity," she snapped, scarlet to the roots of her hair as she pulled away.

"Take care," he said sternly, and bent to retrieve the impractical sandal. "You could have broken your ankle. Put your hand on my shoulder and give me your foot, *Cenerentola*."

Jess complied unwillingly to let him slide on the offending shoe, then bit her lip when Lorenzo took her by the wrists.

He said something brief in his own tongue as he examined the grazed, bleeding palms. "I will take you inside to cleanse your wounds."

"No, *please*," she protested, in an agony of embarrassment. "I'm fine."

Lorenzo shook his head firmly. "You cannot drive with hands which bleed. How far is it to your home?"

"Twenty miles or so—"

"Then I shall drive you. Leave your car here."

"Certainly not," she snapped, then spread her hands wide suddenly as blood threatened to drip on her jacket.

Lorenzi handed her an immaculate handkerchief. "You cannot control a car in this condition. And if you have an accident it will spoil the day for your sister tomorrow."

Unexpectedly hurt by his thought for Leonie rather

than herself, Jess mopped blood and dirt from her grazed palms without looking at him.

"Come," he said imperiously. "I will ask the receptionist for dressings."

Twenty minutes later Lorenzo Forli was driving his mutinous passenger towards Stavely in the car he'd hired for his stay in Britain. "Your hands are still hurting?"

"A little," she muttered, still hot with embarrassment over the fuss made by the assistant manager, who'd been in the foyer when they went back into the hotel. In short order she'd been presented with plasters and antiseptic, offered brandy, and Roberto had been sent for to explain his brother's proposed absence. Roberto's prompt offer to drive Jess to Stavely himself had been summarily dismissed by his brother, and Jess hustled off with only a brief goodnight.

"Perhaps you should have rung Leonie to explain the delay," said Roberto, as he followed her directions to Stavely.

"No need." She said stiffly. "Leo won't be expecting me just yet."

Jess fixed her eyes on the road, cursing the fate which had actually allowed her a meeting with the charismatic stranger, only to find he believed her capable of lusting after her sister's bridegroom. Jess seethed in silence while Lorenzo Forli drove smoothly along the winding road which hugged the river. The scene was very peaceful in the fading light. Later the traffic would increase as Saturday night revellers made for home, but at this hour the journey would have been restful in almost any other circumstances. With Lorenzo Forli at the wheel, however, expert driver though he was, Jess felt anything but restful, consumed with a volcanic mixture of resentment and excitement which made it hard for her to sit still in her seat.

"Why did you run away from me that day?" Lorenzo asked abruptly, startling her. "I think you knew very well I wished to meet you. Was the prospect so intolerable?"

She raised her chin disdainfully.

"It was nothing to do with you, Signor Forli. It was Roberto I was running away from. Because of Jeremy Lonsdale."

"Roberto's friend, the *avvocato*?" He frowned, baffled. "I do not understand."

With resignation Jess once again explained her dilemma as a juror. Lorenzo heard her out, then gave a long smouldering look before returning his attention to the road.

"This does not explain why you refused to speak to *me* when I rang that night."

Jess shot him another startled look. "That was you?"

"Did your friend not tell you?" His expressive mouth tightened. "She said you had the migraine. Was that true?"

"No," said Jess faintly, shaken by the discovery that Lorenzo had rung her on the strength of one fleeting, chance encounter. She cleared her throat. "Emily said it was Signor Forli, so naturally I assumed it was Roberto." She eyed his aloof profile in appeal. "There was another day to go in court so I still couldn't speak to him."

"And if you had known it was I who wished to speak to you? What then?" he demanded, throwing a challenging glance at her.

Jess thought about it for a while. "I'm not sure," she said at last.

Lorenzo's jaw set. "I see."

"I don't think you do. I mean," added Jess in desperation, "that if I had known who you were I would have—

have liked to speak to you, but I'm still not sure whether I would have been breaking any rules if I had.''

He turned to her with a smile of such blatant triumph it took her breath away. ''Ah! That is better. Much better.''

Jess turned away sharply, so floored by her body's response to the smile she spent the next mile or two in pulling herself together, uncertain whether she was sorry or glad when they reached the turning which led past the church and on up to Friars Wood. In command of herself at last, she gave concise instructions as Lorenzo negotiated the steep bends of the drive, telling him to park in front of the Stables, well away from the main house.

''This is my brother's private retreat,'' Jess told him, wincing as she tried to undo the seat belt.

''*Permesso,*'' said Lorenzo, and leaned across her to release the catch, giving her a close-up of thick black lashes and the type of profile seen on Renaissance sculptures. He turned away to get out of the car, and came round to help her out, taking her elbow very carefully. ''I must not hurt your hands. Are they giving you pain?''

''I'm fine,'' she assured him, which was a lie. In actual fact, she felt so weirdly different from usual she was relieved when her brother emerged from the stable block to inject a note of normality.

''Hi, Jess,'' said Adam, eyeing the stranger with curiosity. ''Where's your car?''

''I left it at the Chesterton,'' she explained, and introduced Lorenzo.

''Nice to meet you,'' said Adam as he shook hands.

''*Piacere,*'' said Lorenzo Forli, smiling. ''Your sister fell and hurt her hands, so I drove her home.''

''How the devil did you manage that, Jess?'' demanded Adam. "Don't tell me," he added, resigned, noticing her feet. "Life-threatening heels, as usual."

"I tripped on some gravel," said Jess tersely. "So you'll have to drive me back to Pennington after the wedding, to collect my car."

"No problem," said Adam cheerfully. "Right then, Jess, bring Lorenzo in to meet the family. I was just going to ask Mother to make me a snack."

"You are most kind," said Lorenzo, after a questioning look at Jess's face. "But I will not intrude on this special night."

When it became clear that Lorenzo had no immediate intention of getting back in the car, Adam threw his sister a bright, knowing look, said goodnight, and loped off in search of food.

"Thank you for driving me home," said Jess at last, desperate to break the silence once Adam had gone.

"It was my pleasure." Lorenzo reached out a hand to touch hers. "Jessamy, I can tell that you are angry."

"How perceptive," she snapped, backing away.

"Why?" he asked, advancing on her.

Her head went up. "I would have thought it was obvious. I object to wild accusations about my morals, especially from strangers," she added coldly.

"Ah!" His eyes held hers relentlessly. "We return to the subject of your sister's *fidanzato*. You insist you do not love him?"

"On the contrary, I do," she assured him airily, gratified when his dark eyes blazed with anger.

"You admit this?" he said incredulously.

"Only to you," she said sweetly. "They say it's easier to confide in strangers. So I can share my little secret, Signor Forli."

"Then Roberto was right," said Lorenzo grimly. "He

suspected this when he first met you. No matter. You will be made to change your mind.'' His smile was so arrogant it raised every hackle Jess possessed. ''I swore this the first moment I saw you.''

''But you didn't know who I was.''

He moved closer. ''Ah, but I did.''

Jess stared at him wildly. ''I don't understand.''

''You lie, Jessamy.'' He held her wrists loosely, one finger on her tell-tale pulse.

''I'm not lying,'' she retorted, and pulled her hands away. ''So explain. Had you seen me somewhere before?''

''Only in my dreams,'' he said, routing her completely. He smiled into her eyes. ''But now I've met you in the alluring flesh, Jessamy Dysart, you will forget all other men in your life from this day on, including your sister's husband. I forbid you to gaze at him with longing tomorrow.''

''*What?* You can't *forbid* me to do anything,'' she said, incensed, desperate to hide the tumult of delight beneath her outrage. ''We're complete strangers. I don't know what you think gives you the right to talk to me like this—''

''Why did you cut off your beautiful hair?'' he interrupted, changing the subject with an abruptness which knocked her off balance again.

Jess blinked. ''Not—not quite all of it.''

''Far too much. Almost you look like a boy, now.''

''Do I really!''

''I said almost!'' Lorenzo gave her a slow smile, his eyes lingering on the place where her jacket hung open. ''You are all contradiction, *tesoro*. You wear trousers and cut off your hair, yet choose feminine shoes and a *camicetta* which clings to your breasts. Why can you not glory in the fact that you are a desirable woman? A woman," he added relentlessly, his eyes clashing with hers, "who must no longer yearn for a man forbidden to her."

Jess gave an exclamation of pure frustration, afraid that at any moment the entire Dysart clan would come pouring from the house to press the stranger at their gates to whatever hospitality he would accept. "I don't know why I'm saying this to a man who I'd never met until an hour ago, but I do *not* yearn for Jonah. Nevertheless I've known him for a long time, and it's true that I love him. But like a brother. Or a brother-in-law." She looked him in the eye. "So let's forget all this nonsense, shall we? I'd give you my hand to shake on it, but both of them hurt rather a lot at the moment."

He nodded, his face relaxing visibly. "Very well, we shall talk no more of this." He smiled down at her. "And since we cannot shake hands, English style, we shall say goodnight Italian style—like this." He took her by the shoulders and planted a kiss on both her flushed cheeks. He raised his head to look down at her, no longer smiling, then with an oddly helpless shrug he bent to kiss her mouth, his hands tightening on her shoulders when the kiss went on for a considerable time. He raised his head at last, his eyes slitted. "*Mi scusi!* That was unfair," he said unevenly.

"Unfair?" managed Jess.

"To take advantage when you are injured. But I could not resist." Lorenzo smiled into her dazed eyes, dropped his hands and stood back. "Now, since I cannot see you tomorrow, tell me when you return to London."

"Not for a while."

He moved nearer. "Where are you going?"

"I'm not going anywhere. I'm staying here."

"Then I shall also."

Jess stared at him disbelief.

"You would not like it if I did?" he demanded.

"That's not the point. I don't know you. I just can't believe that you took one look at me that day and decided—"

"That I wanted you," he finished for her.

Jess felt her face flame. "Are you always this direct with women?" she demanded. "Or is this approach commonplace in Florence?"

He shrugged negligently. "I am not concerned with how the other men behave, either in Florence or London. So, Jessamy. When will you be free? Or am I not asking correctly? Should I entreat? Implore? Forgive my lack of English vocabulary. Tell me what to say." He took her by the shoulders again. "Or are *you* saying you have no wish to see me again?"

Jess looked down. "No," she said gruffly. "I'm not saying that."

He put a finger under her chin and smiled down at her in triumph. "Tomorrow, then, after the wedding. You will dine with me."

She shook her head reluctantly. "I can't. I must stay with my family."

"Then Monday."

"Are you staying on that long?"

He bent nearer. "Do you doubt it?" he whispered, and kissed her gently. He raised his head to look into her eyes, muttered something inaudible in his own language and pulled her close, crushing her to him as he kissed her again, no longer gentle, his lips parting hers, his tongue invading, and she responded, shaking, her body curving into his as she answered the demand of the skilful, passionate mouth. For a while Jess was lost to ev-

erything other than the engulfing pleasure of Lorenzo
Forli's kiss. Then she came back to earth abruptly at the
sound of footsteps on the terrace, and pulled away, her
face burning.

Breathing a little rapidly Lorenzo looked up to smile
in greeting when Leonie came hurrying towards them.
"*Buona sera*, Leonie. Please forgive my intrusion."

"Lorenzo, how nice to see you! I couldn't believe it
when Adam said you'd driven Jess home. Roberto didn't
tell me you were here in England with him." Leonie held
up her face and Lorenzo kissed her on both cheeks, sending shamed little pang of jealousy through Jess.

"I joined him only a short time ago. Roberto is here
to visit his friend, but he will return to Florence after
your wedding. I shall stay awhile, and explore your beautiful countryside." Lorenzo glanced at Jess, sending the
colour rushing to her face again. "I was most fortunate,
Leonie, to meet your sister tonight."

"Come and meet the rest of my family as well,
Lorenzo," she said promptly, but he shook his head.

"I must not keep the bride from her beauty sleep." He
smiled at her. "Not, of course, that you need this,
Leonie."

"Thank you, kind sir." She exchanged a look with
Jess, then gave him a cajoling smile. "Lorenzo, feel free
to say no, of course, but since Roberto and Ravellos are
coming to my wedding why don't you come too? It's a
very informal affair. Just a garden party after the church
ceremony tomorrow afternoon. My family would be delighted to welcome you. Wouldn't they, Jess?"

Jess nodded mutely.

Lorenzo's eyes searched her face for a moment, then,
apparently satisfied she approved the idea, he smiled at
Leonie. "You are very kind. I am most happy to accept.

Until tomorrow. *Buona notte!*'' He gave them both a graceful little bow, got back in the car and drove off down the winding drive.

Leonie put an arm round her sister's shoulders and drew her slowly along the terrace to the house. ''Well, well, what have you been up to, sister dear?'' she teased gently. ''I was sent out to invite Lorenzo in, but I beat a hasty retreat when I saw him kiss you. I waited for a bit, but then he started kissing you again, and it seemed unlikely that he was about to stop for the foreseeable future, so I decided to interrupt. Sorry!''

''I tripped and fell in the Chesterton car park and hurt my hands, so he volunteered to drive me home,'' said Jess, flushing.

''With the greatest of pleasure, by the look of it. I don't know Lorenzo as well as Roberto, of course—''

''Obviously,'' retorted Jess. ''You never mentioned him.''

''I haven't met him often. He doesn't socialise much. In fact, Roberto told me that Lorenzo's marriage changed his brother into something of a recluse.''

# CHAPTER THREE

"HE'S married?" Jess stopped dead in her tracks, her world disintegrating about her.

"Renata died about three years ago," said Leonie hastily, bringing Jess back to life. "It was a great shock to Lorenzo. He was married very young, I think. I'm not sure of the details. Actually, I think Roberto's a bit in awe of his older brother, though they see a lot more of each other these days." She gave Jess a sparkling look. "Not that Lorenzo looked much like the grieving widower just now."

"He took me by surprise," muttered Jess as they went in.

Leonie chuckled. "I can see that. You're still in shock!"

Jess shivered a little, and Leonie urged her inside the house.

"Come on I'll make you a hot drink while mother inspects those hands. By the way," she added, "in all the excitement I hope you didn't forget the earrings!"

To the disappointment of Tom Dysart, who rather fancied himself in his father's morning coat and top hat, his daughter had insisted on a very informal wedding. Lounge suits would be worn instead of morning dress for the men. The female guests could splash out on hats. But otherwise she wanted very much the same kind of garden party Jonah's parents had put on in their Hampstead house seven years before, to celebrate their first, ill-fated engagement.

"Only this time," Leonie had declared, "we'll be celebrating a wedding at Friars Wood and nothing will go wrong. The sun will shine, and we'll live happily ever after."

She was right about the weather. The June Sunday was glorious from the start, with just enough breeze to mitigate the heat without endangering the umbrellas shading the tables on the lawn. When the kitchen in the main house was given over to the caterers, quite soon after breakfast, the family moved out into Adam's quarters until it was time to get ready for the main event.

"Rounded up any more guests this morning, Leo?" quizzed Adam, over an early lunch.

"Cheek!" The bride smiled at her mother. "But when I found Lorenzo Forli was here with Roberto it seemed a shame not to ask him. You don't mind, do you, Mother?"

"Not in the least," said Frances placidly. "Numbers don't matter at this kind of thing. And it was very good of him to drive Jess home last night. How on earth did you come to fall like that, darling?"

"Death-defying heels, no doubt," said Tom Dysart. "I hope you're trotting down the aisle in something safer, Jess."

"She has to," said Kate, who measured only an inch or so over five feet. "Today *I'm* in the high heels and Jess is down to something safer to even us out."

"Just make sure *you* don't fall over, then, half-pint," advised her brother.

"As if!" she retorted, giving him a push.

"My shoes don't have any heels at all," said Fenny

with regret, then brightened. "But they've got little yellow rosebuds on the toes."

"Time enough for high heels where you're concerned," said Tom lovingly, then looked at the bride's plate with disapproval. "For pity's sake eat something else, Leo. I can't have you fainting as we march up the aisle."

"No chance," Leonie assured him. "But my dress fits so perfectly I'm leaving the pigging out bit until the wedding feast."

"You're very quiet, Jess," observed her mother. "Are your hands still hurting?"

"Not so much." Jess yawned a little. "I'm just a bit tired after my jury stint, I suppose. Don't worry," she added, "no one will be looking at me today."

"I wouldn't count on that. How about Lorenzo the Magnificent?" said Adam, carving off a sliver of ham with a deft hand. "The man couldn't take his eyes off you last night."

"Rubbish!" Jess made a face at him. "I'd never even met Lorenzo Forli until—until last night."

"So you hadn't," said Leonie, smiling slyly. "Just think how much better you can get to know him today!"

"Talking of today," said Frances, holding out a hand to Fenny, "we'd better get ready. Mrs Briggs will clear away before she sets off for the church, so get a move on everyone. You don't want to be late, Leo."

"Perish the thought," teased Jess, pulling her sister up. "Jonah admitted to nerves last night, so don't keep the poor man waiting on tenterhooks at the altar."

"Don't worry—I'll be punctual to the second."

Leonie was true to her word. Long before it was time to leave the house she was ready, in a slim, unadorned column of ivory slipper satin. Jess secured the pearl brooch into her sister's gleaming hair, handed over the earrings, then stood back to admire the effect.

"How do I look?" she asked.

"Absolutely beautiful," said her mother fondly. "And your bridesmaids do you proud, darling."

Jess and Kate were in bias-cut chiffon the creamy yellow shade of Fenny's layers of organdie, the child in such a state of excitement by this time that Kate had to hold her still for Jess to secure a band of rosebuds on her hair.

The photographer arrived a few minutes later. Frances collected a dramatic straw hat decorated with black ostrich feathers, then herded the entire family off to the drawing room for the indoor pictures. The bride requested the first pose alone with Adam, his lanky frame elegant in a new suit with an Italian label, his mop of black curls severely brushed for once for the photograph, before he rushed off to drive down the lane to the church to do his duty as usher.

Tom Dysart, tall as his son, but with greying hair that had once been flaxen fair as Jess's shining locks, wore a magnificent dark suit with grey brocade waistcoat, and looked as proud as a peacock as he posed, first with the radiant bride, then with his wife, and finally with all his women folk around him.

"Like a sultan in his harem," said Jess, laughing.

"And a damn good-looking bunch you are," said her father fondly.

Later, as Jess waited for the bride with Kate and Fenny in the church porch, she found that her posy was shaking a little in her still tender hand.

"Nervous?" whispered Kate.

"Only of this thing falling out of my hair," lied Jess, controlling an urge to peer into the church to see if Lorenzo had arrived. But it was true that her new haircut,

unlike Kate's flowing dark curls, had made it difficult to
fix the trio of rosebuds attached to a tiny comb. Kate put
her posy down on the porch seat, removed the flowers,
then anchored them again very firmly into one of the
longer gilt strands.

"How's that?"

"Fine, love, thanks. Here we go. The bride's arrived."

Leonie smiled radiantly at her sisters as she glided up
the path, then, to the strains of Mendelssohn, began the
walk up the aisle on her father's arm towards the bridegroom and best man at the altar.

Jonah's tense face relaxed into a smile of such tenderness at the sight of his bride Jess felt her throat thicken,
and dropped her eyes to the flowers she held, as she
walked down the aisle. When they came to a halt she
turned to make sure Fenny was happy behind her and
caught a glimpse of Lorenzo, standing with his brother
towards the rear of the church. She met his eyes for a
long, charged instant, then turned to take charge of
Leonie's flowers as the service began.

When Tom Dysart rejoined his wife after giving his
daughter away, Jonah took Leonie's hand and held it in
his. After the moving ceremony was over the wedding
party moved to the vestry to sign the register, and during
the kissing and congratulations Jess slipped out into the
church to stand beside Helen Savage's wheelchair for a
chat while the organist went through a spectacular rep-
ertoire before launching into Wagner for the triumphal
exit.

Jess hurried back to the vestry and took the best man's
proffered arm, laughing up at Angus Buchanan as he
joked about his terror over his speech. As they drew level
with the Forli brothers Jess surprised such a dark, smouldering look from Lorenzo she realised he was jealous,

and glowed with secret gratification as the wedding party emerged into the sunlight for the inevitable photo session.

Back at Friars Wood, the bride and groom's happiness pervaded the entire scene on the sunlit lawn as they greeted their guests. Everyone milled about with glasses of champagne, laughing and talking, and introducing themselves. First Roberto Forli, then his brother, shook Jonah's hand, and asked smiling permission to kiss the bride. When he reached Jess, to her surprise Roberto saluted her on both cheeks in the same way.

"Lorenzo has told me about your legal problem," he whispered. "I am glad it was not the sight of *my* face which made you run!"

She gave him a wry little smile. "Absolutely not. Jeremy Lonsdale's face did that. Sorry I had to be so rude, Roberto."

"I am sorry also. I should not have said such bad things to you last night." He pulled a face. "Lorenzo was very angry with me when he returned."

"Let's forget it, shall we?" Jess smiled at him warmly, then introduced him to Kate. When Jess turned at last to Lorenzo, he took her hand to draw her closer so that he could kiss both her cheeks.

"You look very beautiful—all woman today," he whispered, and raised a black, quizzical eyebrow. "The best man thought this also, no?"

"Angus is very charming," she said demurely, and gave Lorenzo a smile so radiant his eyes lit up in response. She turned away hastily to welcome Angela and Luigi Ravello. Jess chatted with them for a while, introduced them to other people, then did the rounds of the other guests, all the time finding it a dangerously exciting experience to know that Lorenzo Forli rarely took his eyes from her. This all-out intensity of his was something new in her experience. And gloriously addictive.

Eventually Leonie and Jonah took their places with their respective parents at a table in the centre of the lawn, and Adam and the best man directed guests to the tables grouped casually around the central focus of the bride and groom. Adam wheeled Helen Savage's chair to the nearest table, with Jess and Fenny, and invited the guests from Florence to join them.

Jess made the necessary introductions, and Adam, giving her a surreptitious wink, seated Lorenzo next to her, put Kate between the two brothers, and took his place beside Fenny, who was next to Helen Savage's chair, as she usually was lately, her eyes sparkling as they inspected the tempting canapés and patisserie Leonie had chosen for the meal.

"You obeyed me, Jessamy," said Lorenzo, under cover of the general conversation and laughter.

She eyed him narrowly. "I *obeyed* you?"

"You did not gaze with longing at the bridegroom."

"I should think not," she retorted, looking across at Leonie. "I *told* you how wrong you were about all that. Don't you think the bride looks breathtaking today?" she added.

Lorenzo's eyes followed hers. "Leonie dazzles because she is so happy." He smiled wryly. "Unlike my brother, who was very sad during the ceremony."

Jess glanced at Roberto, who, if he was nursing a broken heart, showed little sign of it as he laughed with Kate. "I'm sure a man like Roberto won't pine unconsoled for long."

"True. Robert leads a very active social life. I," he added very deliberately, "do not." Lorenzo gave her a long, unsmiling look, then noticed Fenny, who was

watching them with interest as she munched on a me-
ringue. "Jessamy, will you introduce me to this very elegant little lady?"

"Of course." Jess smiled affectionately at the youngest bridesmaid. "May I present Miss Fenella Dysart?
Fen, this gentleman's name is Lorenzo Forli."

"How do you do?" said Fenny politely, as she'd been
taught.

"*Piacere,*" said Lorenzo, and got up to kiss her hand.

"Ooh!" Fenny went scarlet with delight. "Did
Mummy see, Jess?"

"Run across and ask her, if you like."

Lorenzo laughed as he watched the little girl race
across the grass. "She will break hearts, that one." Then
his eyes narrowed as he watched Fenny chattering to
Jonah. He frowned. "Strange. Now that I see them together the child greatly resembles the bridegroom. How
can that be?" Colour ran up suddenly beneath his olive
skin. "*Dio*—she is Leonie's child?" he whispered.

"Certainly not!"

Lorenzo turned to look at Jess, his eyes narrowed in
sudden, dark suspicion.

"It's not what you think," she whispered hastily, relieved when Angus Buchanan stood up and put an end
to conversation by tapping his glass for silence. The circumstances of Fenny's birth were complicated, and not
something to discuss with a man who, difficult though it
was for her to remember, was nevertheless still very
much a stranger.

But Jess could sense Lorenzo's preoccupation as the
speeches began. Stranger or not, she found it all too easy
to tell he was brooding beneath the surface. Roberto was
no happier either, she suspected. His smiling mask
slipped a little when Jonah got up to make his speech,

and though Roberto applauded afterwards Jess knew, beyond any doubt, that Roberto Forli would have given much to change places with the bridegroom.

But none of that mattered, Jess reminded herself. Leonie and Jonah were deliriously happy, and deserved to be, after the long years of estrangement they'd suffered before coming together again.

"It was all over so quickly," sighed Leonie afterwards, as she changed for the trip to Paris. "I hope everyone had a good time. I certainly did."

"It's been a beautiful day," Jess assured her.

"Everything was perfect, Leo. So get your skates on—it's time to start the happy-ever-after bit."

"Are you ready, darling?" asked Frances Dysart, coming in. "Jonah's getting a bit impatient down there."

Leonie smiled luminously, then collected her bag and her bridal posy. "Right, then. How do I look?"

"Lovely," said her mother, blinking away a sudden tear as she hugged her daughter carefully. "Mustn't crease that heavenly suit before you start."

Jess kissed her sister's glowing cheek. "Have a wonderful time, Mrs Savage."

"I certainly will!"

The guests had all come up from the lawn to the terrace to see the pair off in the car that Kate, Adam and Angus had festooned with balloons and streamers. With Jonah's arm round her, Leonie tossed her posy into the cheering crowd, where it was caught, much to her astonishment, by Kate.

"No good to me," she said, laughing, "I've got exams to do."

There was a round of kisses and embraces, then cheers as the guests waved the newly-weds off down the drive, and soon afterwards people began to drift away.

"Jessamy," said Lorenzo Forli urgently, when Roberto accompanied the Ravellos to take their leave of Tom and Frances Dysart. "I must talk with you. Is there no way that you can dine with me later?"

"I told you last night that just isn't possible," she whispered. "Jonah's family are staying for a meal with us tonight."

His eyes held hers. "But if I return later tonight, would your family spare you for a little while afterwards? I shall ask them myself, if you permit."

Jess nodded. "If you want to."

"You know very well that I do. Let us join your parents." Lorenzo walked with Jess to thank the Dysarts, and stood talking to them for a while, complimenting them on the perfection of the day. When Tom Dysart was called away, Lorenzo turned to Frances. "It was most kind of you to welcome a stranger to your celebration, Signora Dysart."

"It's always a pleasure to welcome my family's friends," she assured him. "I gather you're returning to London tonight?"

He shook his head. "Roberto is travelling there with our good friends the Ravellos, but I shall stay for a while, and explore this beautiful part of your country."

"Then you must come and visit us again," she said promptly.

"You are most kind. I should be delighted." Lorenzo cast a look at Jess before turning again to her mother. "*Signora*, I was just asking your daughter if you would spare her to me for a while later tonight after you have dined."

"I explained that it was difficult, because of the family supper," said Jess hastily.

Frances Dysart, rarely slow on the uptake, smiled on

them both. "That won't take long, darling. Jonah's family will probably leave early, after all the excitement. Kate and Adam are having some friends over at the Stables to party for a while later, as you know, but you won't fancy that, Jess. If Lorenzo's on his own, by all means keep him company for a while."

After Frances left them to see departing guests on their way Lorenzo looked at Jess urgently. "How soon may I come for you? Is there some quiet place nearby where we can drink a glass of wine together and talk for a while?"

Jess nodded. "But I can't leave before eight-thirty at the earliest. Is that too late?"

"Yes," he said promptly. "Much too late. So when I come you will not keep me waiting, *per favore*."

She gave him a wry, considering look. "I'll try. Now I really must help my parents with the remaining wedding guests. And by his body language I think Roberto wants to leave."

"I have no doubt that he does, now Leonie has departed for her honeymoon. Also he must catch the train for London." Lorenzo raised her hand to his lips. "While I must wait with what patience I can until I see you tonight, Jessamy Dysart. I shall count the minutes. *Arrivederci*."

# CHAPTER FOUR

ALL evening while Jess helped her mother and Kate serve their guests, she found it difficult to concentrate on the buzz of animated post wedding conversation going on around her. She managed to contribute the odd remark now and then, but otherwise she functioned on auto-pilot, hoping her excitement wasn't too obvious as the time drew nearer to Lorenzo's arrival.

"Everything went like a dream today, Frances," said Flora Savage with satisfaction. "You did a fantastic job. Even the weather was perfect."

"Thank God," said Tom Dysart with feeling. "Otherwise everyone would have been crammed into the house."

"Leo was determined to have the reception at home, rain or shine," said Frances serenely. "Which was just as well. The good hotels in these parts need a year's notice for a June wedding."

James Savage chuckled. "Jonah found it hard enough to wait until *this* June once he got Leo back. I don't blame him, either. Your turn next, Jess?"

"Not me," she assured him.

"Leo's Italian friend was very attentive," said Helen casually. "Have you known him long, Jess?"

"She only met him last night," said Adam, grinning.

"Really, dear?" Flora Savage stared in surprise. "I thought you were old friends."

"They soon will be at this rate," said Kate mischievously. "He's taking her out again tonight."

"You mean you're not gracing the Stables with your presence?" demanded Adam.

"And spoil your fun, children? Not a chance." Jess grinned at him, then noticed that Fenny's eyelids were beginning to droop. "Come on, bridesmaid," she coaxed. "Time for bath and bed. I'll take you up tonight."

"But I was going to read Aunt Helen a story," objected Fenny.

"And so you shall," promised Frances. "When you're in your dressing gown you can read to her in the study for a little while."

Once Jess had delivered a clean and shining Fenny into the care of Helen Savage, she raced back upstairs and rushed through a shower, then rummaged frantically through her wardrobe, rattling hangers and discarding one thing after another in a frenzy. Nothing too clingy or sexy, no trousers tonight, something feminine... Suddenly she laughed at herself. Practically anything she'd packed would do for a trip to a country pub, even with Lorenzo Forli.

Eventually, in sleeveless indigo lawn, the skirt of the dress drifting just above her ankles, Jess went downstairs to find that Fenny had fallen fast asleep on the sofa.

"She's had a very exciting day," whispered Helen. "I didn't like to leave her to call someone."

Jess smiled warmly. "I expect you enjoyed a little lull with her on your own."

"I did, indeed." Helen brushed a gentle hand over the dark, shining hair. "She's such a darling."

Also a little enigma that had very plainly disturbed Lorenzo Forli, Jess reminded herself, and went off to get Adam and Kate. "Will you two take Fenny off to bed, while I wheel Helen back to the others?"

"Of course," said Kate, eyeing her sister. "Wow! You look terrific, Jess."

"*Flat* shoes?" said Adam with awe, eyeing his sister's linen sling-backs.

"Only because they match the dress," she assured him.

"You be careful tonight," he said sternly, only half joking.

"I'm careful every night!"

Jess wheeled Helen back to the others, to face a chorus of approval on her appearance, and much kindly teasing from Jonah's parents. Eventually she was rescued by the doorbell, and hurried back along the hall, her heart thumping at the sight of Lorenzo's tall silhouette through the stained glass panels of the inner door. She threw it open, smiling, feeling a rush of reaction at the sight of him. He was less formal tonight, in a lightweight jacket and a shirt open at the throat. And so much everything she'd ever dreamed of in a man she had to swallow before she could speak.

"Hello," she said at last. "You're very punctual."

Lorenzo said nothing for a moment, surveying her with such undisguised pleasure Jess found it hard to stand still.

"*Bellissima,*" he said at last. "But why do you look so small tonight?"

She held up a foot. "Different shoes. Now you see why I like high heels. Would you care to come in for a while?"

"I would like that very much," he said, rather to her surprise. Jess had assumed he would decline politely and whisk her off the first moment he could, as eager to be alone with her as she was with him.

"Would you like a drink?" she asked as she led him to the drawing room.

"Alas, no." He smiled down at her. "I shall wait until later."

The visitor was given a warm welcome. He sat very much at his ease, adding his own comments about the wedding, stressing how privileged he felt to have been a guest. Then, just when Jess thought they could decently take their leave, Kate and Adam joined them, and it was more than half an hour later before Lorenzo got up to go.

"I trust you did not mind that I spent time with your family?" he asked, as he opened the car door for Jess.

"Not in the least." But she did. Just a little.

"I am in your hands, Jessamy," he told her, sliding behind the wheel. "Where shall we go?"

She gave him directions to a country pub a few miles away. "They have a pretty garden there, so perhaps we can sit outside. It's a beautiful evening."

"Very beautiful," he agreed, giving her a swift, all-encompassing glance.

Lorenzo professed himself delighted with the picturesque inn. He led Jess to a rustic bench in the surprisingly deserted garden, then went off to discover the extent of the wine list. The garden was secluded behind high laurel hedges, the scent of roses heavy in the warm summer night, and Lorenzo looked around in surprise as he rejoined her.

"Inside it is very crowded and very hot. Yet this delightful garden is deserted. Not," he added, sitting beside her, "that I complain! And to my surprise they keep a good prosecco here. I hope this pleases you?"

"Perfect," said Jess, who at this particular moment in time would have accepted tap water with equal pleasure. "I'm surprised they keep such a cosmopolitan cellar. I haven't been here for ages."

After a waitress arrived with bottle and glasses, and

departed, smiling, the richer for a generous tip, Lorenzo filled the glasses, then sat back with a sigh of contentment and took Jess's hand in his.

"Ah, Jessamy, this is so perfect."

She smiled up at him. "First of all, Lorenzo, no one uses my proper name. I'm always known as Jess."

He shook his head. "Not to me, *cara*. I shall always call you Jessamy."

Jess saw no point in contradicting him and looked down at their clasped hands, wondering if his reaction to the contact was anything like her own. Which brought her to something she was desperately curious to know. "Lorenzo, can I ask you something?"

"Anything you wish."

"When you first saw me in the pub in London, you seemed to recognise me. How? And no more moonshine about dreams, please."

He laughed. "*Va bene*, I confess. I had seen you in a photograph. When she lived in Firenze Leonie suffered much from *la nostalgia*, I think, and one day she showed me some pictures of your home. You were sitting on the lawn with a large dog, the sun shining on your hair, and those big dark eyes smiling into mine."

"So the first time you saw me," said Jess, feeling a little deflated, "you already knew I was Leo's sister." Not love at first sight after all. Just recognition from a photograph.

Lorenzo smoothed a slim finger over the back of her hand. "It would not have mattered who you were. After only one glimpse of your face in the photograph I could not rest until I met you. When Roberto was invited to Leonie's wedding fate played into my hands. I decided to join him and contrive to meet her sister." He shook his head in wonder. "I could not believe my good fortune when I saw you walk into that London bar. But you ran away before Roberto could introduce us.''

''I've told you why.'' She raised her head and met a look in his eyes which made her pulse race.

''Jessamy,'' he whispered, bending closer. ''You are so charming, so appealing, it amazes me that you have no man in your life.''

''Would you have gone away without meeting me if I had?''

''No.'' He shrugged negligently. ''I knew you had no husband. A lesser relationship would not have deterred me.''

She shook her head, smiling. ''In other words you always get your own way!''

''No.'' His face darkened. ''Not always.''

Jess shivered, cursing herself for her habit of speaking without thinking first.

''You are cold?'' he said swiftly. ''You wish to go inside?''

''No, please.'' Jess looked at him squarely. ''Look, Lorenzo, before you say anything else, I know you were married. Leo told me.''

He nodded, resigned. ''Of course. It is no secret.''

''It must be terrible to lose someone you love,'' she said with sympathy, and shivered again.

''You *are* cold,'' he accused.

''Only a little. But I want to stay here.'' Where they were alone.

''Then there is no alternative.'' Lorenzo put an arm round her and drew her close, and Jess leaned against him as naturally as though they'd sat together like this a hundred times before.

''Will you tell me about your wife?'' she said gently.

He was silent for a time. ''Since she died,'' he said at

last, choosing his words with care, "I have never talked of Renata. But perhaps now it is time that I do. So that there is truth between us, Jessamy."

She tensed, wondering what he meant, and he put a finger under her chin and turned her face up to him.

"You fear what I have to say?"

"No." Jess held his eyes steadily. "I'm a fan of the truth myself."

He nodded in approval, and drew her closer. "First you must know that though I was very fond of Renata, ours was not a love match. Our families were close, and we were brought up almost as brother and sister. I always knew that I was expected to marry her. It was our parents' dearest wish."

"You mean it was an arranged marriage?"

"I was not forced into it. And I believed Renata loved me. I had no choice." He shrugged. "You do not approve of arranged marriages?"

"Absolutely not. If ever I do have a husband I expect to choose him myself!"

His arm tightened. "It is a miracle you are not married already."

"No miracle." She smiled a little. "It's Jonah's fault, really."

Lorenzo stiffened, his eyes suddenly blazing into hers. "What are you saying?"

"Not what you think," she said hastily. "I meant that Jonah met Leo when I was still in school. After seeing them together, so much in love, the way they could hardly bear to be apart for a second, I was determined never to settle for anything less."

He let out an explosive breath. "You take delight in tormenting me."

She leaned closer. "I didn't mean to."

"No?" He raised a quizzical eyebrow, then grew thoughtful. "Jessamy," he said slowly, "are you saying you have never been in love?"

"Yes." She gave him a wry little smile. "I thought I'd come close to it once or twice. But I was mistaken. Both times the gentleman in question went off in a huff, never to return."

"A huff? What is that?"

"Rage, I suppose."

"This I can understand! To believe he is loved and then find he is not—" Lorenzo made a chopping motion with his hand. "This would enrage any man."

"Exactly. So after that I made a conscious decision to wait until I find a death-do-us part kind of thing…" She breathed in sharply in dismay. "Lorenzo—I'm so sorry!"

He shook his head. "Do not apologise, *cara*. I would not have you guard your tongue over every word."

"I thought of you during the ceremony today, wondering if it made you sad."

He raised her hand to his lips, pressing a kiss on it. "It was Roberto who was sad, not I, Jessamy. It is a long time since my own wedding. Sometimes I can almost believe it happened to some other man, not I."

"How old were you?"

"I was twenty-one, Renata was a year younger."

"As young as that!" She hesitated. "Would it be painful to describe her to me?"

Lorenzo was quiet for a while, as though picturing his dead wife in his mind. "Renata had long black hair," he began at last, "and pale blue eyes inherited from some northern ancestor. She was much too thin, with an intensity which seemed to hint at a passionate nature. We were married with all the usual ceremony in a church full of lilies. And later that night," he added with sudden bitterness, "my bride became hysterical with fear when I tried to consummate our marriage."

Jess stared at him in horror. "But you said she loved you."

"She did. In her way. But this was not as a wife loves a husband." Lorenzo stared unseeingly into the scented twilight. "Renata had no wish to be wife to any man. That night, once she was sure I would not force her, she confessed she had always longed to enter a convent. Her parents forbade this." He shrugged. "They were elderly, Renata was their only child, and a loving, obedient daughter, so she surrendered to their wishes. Which was disaster for both of us."

"That's so sad," said Jess huskily. She hesitated. "Did—did things ever improve?"

"If you talk of a normal married relationship, no." Lorenzo shrugged. "Do not mistake me, Jessamy. I was fond of Renata. I would have done my best to make her happy and give her children. But all hope of that died on our wedding night, killed by her frenzied rejection. We were both trapped by our marriage vows. So. We agreed to act out our pathetic little *commedia*, and keep the true state of our marriage secret. When my unsuspecting parents died, years later, their only regret was the lack of grandchildren."

There was a sudden eruption of people from the hotel, accompanied by a burst of laughter as they made for the car park. Jess stirred instinctively, but Lorenzo held her fast.

"Did Roberto know the truth?" she asked, settling back against him.

Lorenzo shrugged. "He knew that my marriage was not—not perfect. But for many reasons I have never told him the truth."

Jess stared down at their clasped hands. "It must have been so hard for a man like you," she said with difficulty.

"A man like me?"

"Lorenzo, you know very well what I mean. You're a healthy, virile male. A marriage like yours must have been hell for you."

"In that way it was." He rubbed his cheek over her hair. "During my marriage my pride prevented me from seeking consolation elsewhere, you understand. But afterwards," he added carefully, "when certain privileges were offered I have not refused."

"You mean that if a woman gives out certain signals you don't fight her off!" teased Jess, in an effort to lighten the atmosphere.

He laughed a little. "I am expressing myself in a foreign language, remember."

"And very well you do it," she assured him.

"Good. Because there must be no misunderstandings between us, Jessamy. Now or in the future."

Jess peered up at him uncertainly in the gathering dusk, her heart racing at his mention of the future.

"What is it, *carissima*?" he asked softly.

She tried to laugh, make light of it. "Now and then I get this little attack of unreality."

"Make no mistake," he said fiercely. "This *is* reality, Jessamy. Since my marriage I have never felt truly alive until now."

Jess trembled, and he put his other arm round her.

"I should not keep you out here like this."

"I'm not cold," she blurted. "It's just the effect you have on me."

Lorenzo was utterly still for an instant, then he crushed her close and kissed her with a tender ferocity which sent shock waves through her entire body. "Do you know what it means to me to hear you say such things, *amore*?'' he demanded raggedly, raising his head at last. ''Forgive me, Jessamy, this is a public place—''

''I don't care,'' she said recklessly, and kissed him back.

Lorenzo responded without reserve, his body shaking with the intensity of the feelings she'd aroused, and Jess exulted, proud of her power. Then he gave a groan like a man in pain and dropped his arms. ''We must go,'' he panted. ''Now!''

Jess took the hand he held out to her and stood up, then saw the untouched glasses of wine on the table, the half-full bottle beside them. ''Lorenzo! What a terrible waste. I forgot all about the wine.''

''And why did you forget?'' he demanded, his fingers tightening on hers.

''I was too wrapped up in you,'' she said gruffly.

Lorenzo said something unintelligible in his own tongue and pulled her into his arms to kiss her at such length they were both speechless when he let her go. Without another word he took her by the hand and led her to the car, neither of them saying another word during the journey to Stavely. Inside the car the tension between them mounted to such heights Jess could hardly breathe by the time Lorenzo turned up the lane which led to Friars Wood. Suddenly he stood on the brakes, and she saw a cat streak across the lane, a blur of pale fur in the headlights.

''*Scusa,*'' said Lorenzo through his teeth. He drove on at a snail's pace, then stopped the car under a tree which shaded a spot wide enough to park. He wrenched his seat belt free, then reached over to release Jess and pulled her into his arms like a man at the end of his tether. He kissed her with a barely suppressed frenzy she responded to

equally fiercely, and it was a long time before he raised
his head to gaze down into her dazed, heavy eyes.

"Forgive me, *amore*," he said, in a tone which melted
her very bones.

"For what?"

"For making love to you in a car, like some callow
Romeo." His wide, sensuous mouth curved in self-
mockery. "You give me back my youth, Jessamy. I have
no defence against my desire for you."

"How old *are* you?" she demanded.

"Thirty-four."

"I thought you were older than that."

He drew back, eyeing her ruefully. "I look so ancient?"

"Not ancient—mature!" She pulled his head down to
hers and kissed him hard, then rubbed her cheek against
his.

He shrugged wryly. "I learned maturity very early."

Jess ached with sympathy. "Which is why you seem
so assured, I suppose, so much in control."

"In control!" He gave a breathless laugh. "With you
I am twenty again, with no control at all." He trailed his
lips over her eyelids and down her cheeks, pressing light,
tantalising kisses which left Jess wanting more. She
wound her arms round his neck, kissing him with a passion she'd never known she was capable of, and reaped
a reward which transcended anything she'd ever imagined.

It was a long time before Lorenzo let her go. "Tomorrow," he panted at last. "How soon can we meet?"

"How early do you want me—?" She bit her lip as
he laughed deep in his throat.

"I want you now, Jessamy. So much I ache with longing. You know this." He kissed her nose and settled her

back in her seat, reaching over to do up the seat belt. When it was fastened he stayed arched over her, looking down into her eyes. "If I come early in the morning, would your family find this strange?"

Jess gave him a demure little smile. "How early?"

"Ten?"

"Done. What do you want to do?"

"I have come to explore your beautiful countryside, so you shall be my guide. We shall spend the day together." He stretched out a hand to the ignition key, but Jess put a hand on his arm.

"Don't start the car yet. Before we get back there's something I forgot to tell you."

"What is it?" he demanded, his voice harsh with sudden tension.

"I meant to bring the subject up earlier," said Jess ruefully, "but it—it went out of my head."

"What is this subject?" he asked very quietly.

"This afternoon, at the reception, you were a bit remote after you saw Fenny with Jonah."

Lorenzo let out a deep breath, and settled back in his seat.

Jess could tell he was relieved. What had he expected her to say?

"I was a jealous fool," he said with remorse. "I soon realised that the child could not be yours. Forgive me, Jessamy, I had no right to intrude on something so personal to your family."

"I knew you were coming to all the wrong conclusions, so after you left this afternoon I asked permission to tell you Fen's history." Jess sighed. "Poor unsuspecting mite—she's caused enough trouble already."

"Trouble?" queried Lorenzo, frowning. "In what way?"

"Leo broke her engagement to Jonah all those years ago because she thought he was the unborn Fenny's father."

*"Dio!"* he said, startled.

"My father's sister Rachel was in her early forties, working as personal assistant to Jonah's father, when she met the love of her life at last. Leo overheard Rachel telling Jonah she was pregnant, begging him never to reveal the truth to her. She assumed he was the father, of course, flew back to Italy, and broke up with Jonah, refusing to give any explanation. And because Rachel was Dad's much-loved sister Leo couldn't tell my parents why, either."

Lorenzo shook his head in amazement. "I confess I am curious." He eyed her questioningly. "Who *is* the little one's father?"

"Richard Savage, Jonah's uncle. You met Richard's wife, Helen, today. She was the one Rachel was desperate not to hurt, not Leo." Jess sighed. "Richard looked a lot like Jonah, especially the hazel eyes he handed down to Fenny."

Lorenzo smoothed a caressing hand down her cheek. "Will you forgive me for my wild imaginings, Jessamy?"

She smiled wryly. "Wild imaginings are right. Jonah never had eyes for anyone other than Leo from the first moment they met."

"This I can believe!"

"She's beautiful, isn't she?"

"True." He lifted her hand to her mouth. "But you mistake me. I also know how one look is enough to recognise one's fate."

Jess looked away, her heart thumping, and went on with her story. "Helen's brain tumour resulted in paralysis, which ended the physical side of her marriage, but Richard never looked at another woman until he fell madly in love with Rachel. He was killed in a car accident before she could tell him she was pregnant. Rachel was so heartbroken she died giving birth to Fenny.''

Lorenzo flinched. *"Che tragedia!''* he said harshly. "Does the little one know this?''

"No. Not yet. My parents intend telling her as soon as she's old enough to understand.''

"And for one crazy moment I suspected you, Jessamy!'' Lorenzo threw out his hands in appeal. "Forgive me, *tesoro*. I have not experienced jealousy before. It seems it deprives a man of his wits.''

Jess smiled at him, beginning to think she could forgive this man anything. "It's late. Time I was home.''

"You are right. I have no wish to anger your charming parents. It is most necessary that they approve of me.''

"Why?''

Lorenzo smiled into her eyes. "I think you know the answer very well, Jessamy Dysart.''

When they arrived at Friars Wood, to the sound of music thumping from the Stables, Jess exclaimed in surprise when Adam came hurtling from the party to intercept them.

"Sorry to interrupt,'' he panted.

"What's wrong?'' demanded Jess in alarm. "Not Leo—?''

"No, it's your pal Emily. She rang from Florence about an hour ago. In a right old state, apparently. Mother's hoping you can help out, Lorenzo.''

# CHAPTER FIVE

TOM DYSART opened the door to them in obvious relief. "Come in, come in, Lorenzo. Are we glad to see you. If we'd known where you were, Jess, we'd have contacted you before."

"What on earth's happened, Dad?" said Jess anxiously. "Is it something to do with Emily's sister?"

"No, darling," said Frances. "Celia never made it after all. The children went down with chicken pox."

Jess eyed her in consternation. "Emily's on her *own*? Don't say she's had an accident!"

"No, no, nothing like that. She's feeling very unwell, poor dear."

"In what way can I help, *signora*?" asked Lorenzo swiftly.

Frances smiled at him gratefully and handed him a card with a number. "Would you ring the hotel and find out what help we can arrange for Emily?"

"I'd have had a shot at it myself if it had been France," said Tom apologetically. "I could have managed in French—just. But not Italian."

"First, I think, Jessamy must speak with her friend and discover the problem." Lorenzo keyed in the number, waited for a while, then conducted a quick-fire exchange in Italian and handed the receiver to Jess. "They are putting you through to your friend's room."

Jess waited a moment, then heard her friend's hoarse, fearful response.

"Hi, Em," she said quickly. "It's me, Jess. What's the matter, love?"

"*Jess*! Oh, Jess, thank heavens. I'm so glad to hear your voice." Emily broke off to cough. "Sorry to make a fuss like this," she gasped, "but I feel ghastly. I'm so hot, and I've got this terrible pain."

Jess blenched. "Have you rung the desk to ask for a doctor?" she demanded.

"It's the middle of the night. I didn't like to—" Emily broke off into painful coughing again, and dissolved into tears.

"All right, love, all right," soothed Jess. "Don't cry, Em. Hang in there. Listen, I'll get the first flight I can, I promise, so you won't be on your own for long. I'll be in Florence before you know it. In the meantime Lorenzo will organise things from this end, and get a doctor to see you right away."

"Who's Lorenzo?" croaked her friend.

"I'll explain later. Must ring off now, to let him get on with it."

When Jess explained Emily's symptoms Lorenzo took the phone from her swiftly. "I shall arrange for a doctor at once."

Jess shuddered at the thought of her friend alone and ill in a strange country. But as she listened to Lorenzo's flow of musical, expressive Italian she had to fight down a guilty pang of disappointment. There would be no idyll with Lorenzo after all.

Lorenzo finally gave the Dysart telephone number, reiterated his thanks, then rang off and turned to the others. "I was fortunate to get through to my own doctor, Bruno Tosti. He is a personal friend, and will go immediately to the hotel." He smiled reassuringly at Jess. "Do not worry. Bruno speaks English. Your friend is in good hands. The hotel will report here to me on his diagnosis.''

"Wonderful! Thank you so much, Lorenzo," said Frances in relief. "Will they really ring back from the hotel at this time of night?"

"But of course, *signora*." He smiled a little. "The hotel is part of the group run by my family."

"Ah! Splendid," said Tom Dysart, relieved. "That's a load off my mind."

"While you're waiting I'll make some coffee and a few sandwiches," said Frances, looking happier. "You hardly ate a thing at dinner tonight, Jess. Come and help me, Tom."

Jess took Lorenzo into the comfortably shabby study, smiling at him with heartfelt gratitude. "I don't know how to thank you, Lorenzo——"

"I know a very good way," he said promptly, and took her in his arms to kiss her. "This is all I need," he muttered against her mouth. He raised his head, his dark eyes gleaming as they gazed down into hers. "I would do anything in the world for you, Jessamy. Never doubt this."

In her dealings with the opposite sex shyness had never been a problem for Jess. But Lorenzo's words deprived her of speech.

"You said you like the truth," he reminded her.

"I know." She smiled shakily. "It's my unreality problem again."

Lorenzo smiled indulgently. "I know ways to cure this, but not here, not now." He frowned. "Your mother said you did not eat tonight. Why?"

"I was too excited," she admitted, flushing.

"Jessamy!" He made an instinctive move towards her,

then halted, smiling ruefully, as he heard her parents returning.

"If you don't mind," said Tom Dysart, setting a tray down, "we'll turn in now. It's been quite a day, one way and another. Kate's in bed, by the way, Jess, and the party should break up soon. But we insist you stay the night, Lorenzo."

"Absolutely," said Frances firmly. "We can't have you driving back to Pennington in the small hours. Adam's old room is always ready for visitors."

Lorenzo smiled with gratitude. "This is most kind. I thank you both."

"The least we can do," Tom assured him. "Right, then, we'll leave you to it. Jess will show you where to sleep. And thanks again, Lorenzo. You've been a great help."

"*Prego*. I am only too glad."

When the goodnights had been said, and they were alone again Lorenzo took Jess by the hand and sat down with her on the sofa, smiling a little. "I am very sorry that your friend is ill, *carissima*, but secretly I cannot help feeling grateful to her. Otherwise we should not be sitting here alone together at this time of night."

"True." Jess sighed guiltily. "Poor Emily. I just hope it's nothing serious."

"Bruno will do everything necessary, I promise," Lorenzo assured her. "Now. You must eat."

"But—"

"I insist." He wagged a reproving finger at her. "Or I shall feed you, mouthful by mouthful—" Sudden heat flared in his eyes, and he blinked and turned away. "*Dio*, it seems I cannot be trusted. I must sit somewhere else."

"No. Please." Jess caught his hand. "Let's have some

coffee. Or would you prefer wine, since we never got round to the prosecco?''

"*Grazie*, no," he said firmly, "Just to be close to you like this intoxicates me enough!''

"Then we'll both be sensible and drink coffee." Jess eyed him cajolingly. "Please eat a sandwich, Lorenzo, or Mother will be offended.''

"I repeat, Jessamy," he said huskily. "For you I would do anything.''

A statement which made it very hard for Jess to apply herself to a sandwich she didn't want. Nothing, short of measles and the odd bout of flu, had ever deprived her of her appetite in her entire life. This was new. She finished her coffee in sudden dejection.

"What is it, Jessamy?" he said quickly.

"We won't have our day together after all. I must get to Florence as soon as I possibly can." She got up to put cups and plates on the tray.

"There will be other days." Lorenzo drew her down beside him. He put an arm round her and drew her close, his cheek on her hair. For a moment or two they sat quietly, savouring each other's nearness, but at last Lorenzo gave a deep sigh and turned her face up to his. "It is no use, *amore*, I cannot hold you without wanting to kiss and caress—"

The phone cut off the rest of his words, and with a muffled oath Lorenzo seized it from the table beside him and barked his name. He listened intently for some time, asked some questions, then spoke afterwards at length, and put the phone down.

"What did they say?" demanded Jess.

"Your friend is suffering from *la pleurite*, I think you call this pleurisy.''

Jess eyed him in consternation, then made for the

bookshelves along the wall and took down a medical dictionary to leaf quickly through the pages. "Inflammation of the pleura," she reported. "The thin membrane round the lungs. Pain caused by deep breaths or coughing. What a thing to happen on holiday alone! Emily can't speak a word of Italian. Did they mention treatment?"

"She has been given antibiotics and something to make her sleep. Bruno is arranging for a nurse to come immediately, and suggests you ring your friend in the morning." Lorenzo smiled caressingly. "There, Jessamy. Do you feel better now?"

"Much better!" She leaned over the arm of the sofa to kiss him, and he pulled her down beside him, returning the kiss with a hunger she responded to without reserve. After the anxiety of the past hour her relief swiftly changed to desire as she felt Lorenzo's heart thudding through the thin material of her dress. The rhythm accelerated when her lips closed in welcome over his seeking tongue, but at last he held her away a little, his eyes dilating as they dropped to her turbulent breasts. With a smothered groan he caressed the pointing nipples through their filmy covering, and kissed her parted mouth with a passion she responded to in total abandon.

At last Lorenzo drew away, his hands cupping her flushed face. "You set me ablaze, Jessamy," he said unevenly. "But you must believe that it was not for this that I travelled to England to see you."

"What did you expect, then?"

"To meet you, and to get to know you at least a little. But even in my dreams I never aspired to such delight as this—nor such torment!"

"Neither did I," she said with feeling. "It's all so new it's frightening."

His eyes narrowed in incredulous question.

She smiled a little. "Whatever this is that happens between us has never happened for me before."

"*Carissima*!" Lorenzo seized her in his arms and kissed her again, but this time with such protective tenderness Jess relaxed against him like a tired child, suddenly exhausted. "Come," he said, and stood up, holding out his hand. "You must sleep." He smiled at her. "Is your brother's room close to yours?"

"Next door," she said, turning out lights.

Lorenzo sighed heavily. "Then I will probably not sleep at all."

Jess was up early the following morning, but Lorenzo was before her. She went into the kitchen to find him eating breakfast with her family, looking very much at home.

"*Buon giorno*!" he said, jumping up to pull out a chair. "How are you this morning, Jessamy?"

"Tired." She flushed as she met interested looks on all sides.

"Lorenzo told us about Emily's pleurisy, Jess," said Kate. "How awful for her! Mother says you're going out to join her as soon as you can."

"You'd better get on the phone straight after breakfast," said her father. "Could be tricky getting a flight this time of year."

"Have no fear, Signor Dysart, I shall arrange all that," said Lorenzo at once, and passed a jug of orange juice to Jess. "Drink a little of this, *cara*. It will revive you."

Jess sipped obediently, feeling her colour deepen under Kate's fascinated gaze.

"Lorenzo lives in Italy, Jess," announced Fenny, impressed. "Just like Leo did."

"I know, poppet."

"Is that a long way?"

"Two hours only in an aeroplane," Lorenzo informed her, smiling.

"Is your house big?"

"Big enough, *piccola*. You must come and visit me there one day."

"Yes, please!" Fenny nodded with enthusiasm. "Kate and Adam, too?"

"Of course," he assured her gravely.

"Honestly, Fen," said Kate, embarrassed. "Come *on*, we'll be late. Are you ready, Dad?"

Tom Dysart downed the last of his coffee and stood up. Lorenzo followed suit to shake hands. Thanks were exchanged and there was a round of hugs and kisses—Fenny not at all pleased when she heard Jess might not be there when she got back from school.

"Fenny thinks we should all live here all the time, with no going away to college and jobs and so on," explained Frances, after her husband had taken his daughters off.

"And who can blame her?" said Lorenzo. "This is a beautiful part of the world."

"So is yours," said Jess.

"You have eaten nothing, *cara*," he accused.

"Come on, Jess, this isn't like you," said her mother. "Have some toast, at least."

"And while you eat your breakfast, *signora*, with your permission I shall make use of the telephone," said Lorenzo.

"Of course. Use the one in the study." When he'd gone Frances looked at her daughter in wry amusement as she passed the toast. "You're very quiet."

"Just tired," said Jess, with a yawn.

"Were you late getting to bed?"

"Very. It took ages for Lorenzo to get things sorted out."

"He told us. Poor Emily. What a thing to happen alone on holiday!"

"Do you think I should ring her mother?" asked Jess, frowning.

Frances thought for a moment. "I should wait until you see Emily. Let her decide. If Mrs Shaw is involved with the chicken pox she has more than enough to cope with already, poor dear."

Breakfast had been cleared away, and Frances had gone over to the Stables to rouse Adam by the time Lorenzo returned to the kitchen to report.

"It took some time to get through this morning, Jessamy. But eventually I spoke to the nurse, who said your friend is improving."

"Thank heavens for that," said Jess in relief. "I'll ring through in a minute and speak to Emily myself."

"She is now sleeping, therefore I told the nurse you would be with your friend later today," he informed her.

"Have you arranged a flight, then?" she said, surprised.

Lorenzo smiled. "But of course. Your plane leaves Heathrow this afternoon. Do you need much time to pack, *cara*?"

"No, I did that last night." Jess smiled a little. "One way and another I just couldn't get to sleep. I should imagine you did better after all that telephoning."

Lorenzo shook his head, and touched a finger to the curve of her bottom lip. "How could I sleep? When you were so close, but not close enough!" He frowned suddenly. "But I regret that I have added much to your father's phone bill."

''Don't offer to pay! Not if you want to come here again—'' She halted, flushing, and he smiled indulgently.

''You know very well that I do.''

''I'm sure they'll be delighted to see you any time during your stay,'' said Jess forlornly.

He stared at her in amazement. ''But I am not staying, Jessamy. What possible reason could I have for remaining here if you are in Firenze? I travel with you.''

Travel with Lorenzo Forli was very different from anything Jess had experienced before. After Lorenzo's farewells she had submitted to Adam's bear hug, reminded him to fetch her car, then kissed her mother goodbye and rushed out to the car with Lorenzo to drive to Pennington for his luggage before going on to Heathrow to catch the plane.

In a remarkably short time, it seemed to Jess, they were in the sky, bound for Italy. Air travel was normally an evil she endured as the quickest way to get from one point to another. But travelling first class with Lorenzo had a magic carpet quality about it. Sitting close to him, her hand in his, Jess found herself enjoying the entire process for the first time, so absorbed in his company she had no attention to spare for the food they were served.

''It is my ambition to see you eat something one day,'' he observed, resigned, after the trays were removed.

''Normally I eat like a horse,'' she assured him. ''The last few days have been a bit hectic, that's all, with the wedding straight on top of my jury duty, and now this with poor Emily.''

''Try not to worry—you will soon be with her. Instead tell me more about your jury service. Did you enjoy this?'' he asked, reaching for her hand again.

''Not enjoy, exactly. But I'm glad, now, that I did it.''

Lorenzo frowned. "It occurs to me, regrettably late, Jessamy, that I have told you many things I have confided to no one. Yet I have asked nothing about the work you do. Forgive me, *cara*. Are you a teacher, like Leonie?"

Jess pulled a face. "No, not my scene at all. I'm a booker in a model agency."

"A booker?" he said, puzzled. "What is this?"

"I book the models for a London agency. I work with the chief scout, help with new faces, deal with their anxious parents and so on. But actually I prefer my work with the older models, who tend to be more relaxed than the young ones."

Lorenzo looked surprised. "But I thought models must always be very young, also very thin."

"They are, mostly. But modelling isn't just catwalks and glossy magazines. It involves a lot of advertising and catalogue work, which is where the more mature ladies come into their own."

"Have you done modelling yourself, Jessamy?"

She laughed. "No way. Not my sort of thing. Besides, I've never had the right shape for the catwalk, and I'm not old enough yet to promote anti-wrinkle cream."

"Your skin is flawless, and I think your shape is perfect," he whispered, and leaned closer. "I would like very much to kiss you right now, *carissima*, but I think you would not like that."

"Oh, yes, I would," she said in his ear. "But I'd rather be kissed in private."

"I will remind you of that later!"

She suppressed a shiver at the mere thought of it, and changed the subject. "You haven't told me how you managed to get a flight so easily."

"I told Roberto to transfer his reservation to you. He

will stay on with his friend the *avvocato* until he can reserve another.''

"Goodness," said Jess, impressed. "Does Roberto always jump when you tell him to?''

"Always," Lorenzo assured her.

"But what about *your* ticket?''

He smiled smugly. "I already had one.''

"Oh. I see." She smiled, enlightened. "You were all prepared to fly home with Roberto if I'd been a disappointment!''

"You are wrong, *tesoro*. I knew in my heart that you would be all I had ever hoped for." He shrugged. "However, it was possible that you might not have liked *me*.''

"I find that hard to imagine," she said involuntarily, and caught her breath as she saw his eyes dilate.

"If you do not wish me to kiss you here and now," he said through his teeth, "it is best you do not say such things.''

"It's the truth, Lorenzo.''

He raised her hand to his lips and pressed a kiss into the palm. "I begin to suffer from this unreality of yours. When I think of my past loneliness—" He breathed in deeply, and smiled with such tenderness Jess felt her throat thicken. "You know that when I first saw your face in the photograph I vowed I would do everything in my power to meet you. But I did not recognise you then.''

She eyed him questioningly. "You knew who I was.''

"True. " He frowned in concentration. "How I wish you spoke my language, Jessamy, so that I could make my meaning clear. What I try to say is now I have met you at last, I know *what* you are.''

"What I am?" repeated Jess, eyes narrowed.

He nodded triumphantly. "You are my reward!''

# CHAPTER SIX

WHEN Jess arrived in the hotel room her heart contracted at the first glimpse of her friend. The brown glossy hair Emily took such care of hung lank around her face, and streaks of hectic colour along her cheekbones contrasted alarmingly with her pallor.

"*Jess!* Oh, Jess—you came!" Emily's sunken grey eyes lit up with pure relief, then brimmed over with tears when her friend gave her a careful hug.

"My word, Em," Jess teased, sitting on the edge of the bed. "If you're improving I dread to think what you looked like before!"

Emily accepted the wad of tissues a motherly little nurse handed her, and mopped herself up. "Think Bride of Frankenstein," she said hoarsely, and sniffed hard, doing her best to smile. "I should have rung my mother, not you, Jess, I know, but I hated the thought of scaring her silly until I knew what was wrong with me. Sorry to be such a nuisance."

"Rubbish," said Jess fiercely, needing to sniff a little herself. "Due to Lorenzo I was the best one to contact, anyway." She stood up and held out her hand to the hovering nurse. "Hello. I'm Jess Dysart. Thank you so much for looking after my friend."

"*Piacere,*" said the woman, smiling cheerfully. "I am glad to be of service."

"Sorry!" said Emily in remorse. "I'm forgetting my manners. Jess, this is Anna, my angel of mercy. She's been so kind."

"I can see you're in good hands." Jess smiled warmly at the nurse. "Signor Forli would like a word with you, Nurse. He's waiting in the lobby."

"And while you're away please take a break, Anna," said Emily quickly. "Have some coffee and a rest. You deserve it."

Anna nodded, smiling. "*Va bene.* Now your friend is here I shall leave you together for half an hour."

"Lorenzo obviously wants to ask her if you need anything," said Jess, when they were alone.

"Who on earth *is* this Lorenzo?" said Emily, struggling to sit up.

"Hang on, I'll prop your pillows up."

"Never mind my pillows! This morning *that* arrived." Emily waved a hand at the vast basket of fruit on the dressing table. "And after you rang last night masses of mineral water and fruit juice arrived for me. Then Dr Tosti came, with Anna. He's very nice, and speaks English, thank heavens. He gave me an examination, assured me I wasn't dying, and prescribed some antibiotics. Then he left Anna behind to take care of me. So tell. Who is this Lorenzo?"

"Oddly enough," said Jess casually, "you've already spoken to him."

"I have?"

"That night at the flat. He's the one with the sexy voice you fancied so much."

Emily stared in astonishment. "But I thought that was Roberto!"

"No." Jess stretched luxuriously. "It was Lorenzo Forli, Roberto's older brother, chairman of the group that owns this hotel." She paused, then gave her friend a wry, crooked little smile. "But much more important than that, he's the man I'm truly, madly, deeply in love with."

Emily flopped back against the pillows, pole-axed. "You're serious!" she accused, heaved in a deep breath and began to cough painfully.

Alarmed, Jess handed her a glass of water. "Hey— steady on, love."

Emily swallowed the water, then waved a peremptory arm at the other bed. "Right then, Jess Dysart," she ordered. "You can't stop there. Curl up on that and tell me everything. Right from the beginning."

Jess was only too happy to oblige, from the fall at the Chesterton, which had resulted in the drive home to Friars Wood with Lorenzo, to the flight he'd arranged to bring her rushing to Emily's aid. "And as the icing on the cake," she added with satisfaction, "the moment you're well enough for a car ride, Em, he's taking us to stay at his home in the country. I'll keep you company there while you get yourself better."

"How *kind* of him!" Emily shook her head in wonder. "He must be some man, this Lorenzo."

"He is." Jess swung her legs over the edge of the bed and leaned forward, suddenly serious. "Now then, Em. Have you rung your mother?"

"I spoke to her as soon as I arrived, but didn't let on I was feeling rough—told her the flight had made my voice dry." She eyed Jess guiltily. "The thing is, love, when Celia had to cancel I knew perfectly well I should have done the same. I'd been feeling a bit off for a day or two before I left."

"Which is why you were home early that day!" Jess bit her lip in remorse. "And I was too wrapped up in my own concerns to notice."

"I didn't feel so bad then, Jess. I just thought I had a cold coming on. But I was utterly determined to get to Florence. Serves me right, I suppose, because I just wanted to crawl into bed and die by the time I finally got to the hotel.''

When the nurse returned she had a message from Lorenzo. ''Signor Forli wishes to speak to you, Miss Dysart. He awaits you downstairs.''

''On your mark, get set, then, Jess,'' said Emily, grinning. ''Don't keep the man waiting.''

Jess flushed, her eyes like stars as she flew to the bathroom to tidy up. ''Shan't be long,'' she said breathlessly, as she hurried from the room.

When the lift doors opened into the lobby Lorenzo was waiting for her. Aware of rapt attention from everyone behind the reception desk, Jess returned his greeting sedately, then accompanied him to a large lounge, where they sat on a brocade sofa screened by a vast palm, with coffee on a silver tray on the table in front of them.

''*Allora*, how is your friend?'' asked Lorenzo.

''She's not very well at all,'' Jess handed him his cup. ''In fact she looks terrible. But Emily assures me she's much better than she was.''

''I have been speaking to Bruno Tosti, and he confirms this, but he thinks it best your friend remains here for tonight. Tomorrow I will drive you both to the Villa Fortuna.'' Lorenzo smiled at her. ''I have sent word for everything to be made ready.''

''Where exactly is the house?'' asked Jess.

''A short journey from Firenze—it should not be too exhausting for your friend.''

''Do you commute into the city every day, then?''

''No. I have an apartment here. I use the villa only at weekends.'' He lowered his voice. ''But while you are there, *tesoro*, I shall remain there also. Roberto will return tomorrow, or the next day. He can take my place for a while.'' He moved closer, and touched her hand fleetingly. "What is it, Jessamy? Something troubles you."

She shook her head. "Not troubles, exactly. It's just that I'm totally overwhelmed by your kindness, Lorenzo—Emily, too."

He shrugged negligently. "It is no great thing. Later this evening, when I collect you for dinner, you shall present me to your friend."

Jess raised a mocking eyebrow. "So I'm having dinner with you, am I?"

Lorenzo smiled indulgently. "But of course. When you return to your friend, Anna can take time to herself for an hour or two. She will return at eight. You look doubtful," he added, eyes narrowed. "You do not wish this?"

"You know I do," she assured him. "But I'd rather not go too far, Lorenzo, just in case Emily wants me."

"Of course. We shall dine here in the hotel, *cara*. You could be with your friend in minutes, should this be necessary, I shall come for you at eight." Lorenzo escorted her to the lift, bowing very formally as the doors closed on her.

When Jess got back to the room Emily was sitting in a chair, looking tired, but a lot more like herself in a fresh nightgown, with her hair brushed into something more like its normal shine.

"Anna's given me a sponge bath and changed the bed," she said cheerfully. "Then she's going off for an hour or so."

The nurse helped Emily back into bed, and straightened the bedclothes with precision. "I have ordered a light meal, *cara*, and your friend must make sure you eat

it,'' she said firmly, and gathered up the discarded linen.
''I shall return at eight. *A presto!*''

Jess saw the nurse out, then returned to sit on the other
bed. ''Lorenzo wants me to have dinner with him, Em.''

''I know. Anna told me.''

''Do you mind terribly?'' Jess pulled a face. ''I feel a
bit guilty flying to your side and all that, then leaving
you alone for the evening.''

''Of course I don't mind,'' said Emily, chuckling.
''Besides, I won't be alone. I'll have Anna. She can
snooze on your bed while I read.''

''Which reminds me.'' Jess dived for her luggage, and
produced two paperback novels. ''I bought these at the
airport. One thriller, one sexy romance.''

Emily beamed. ''Wonderful! So what are you wearing
for your romantic dinner for two, then?''

''We're on the move tomorrow, so there's no point in
unpacking.'' Jess took out a dress and held it up, eyeing
it critically. ''This knitted silky stuff travels well. I
packed in such a terrible hurry nothing else is fit to be
seen. I'll hang it on the bathroom door to get the creases
out. But first I'm going out on that balcony to look at the
view!''

Outside the full moon was just rising over the Arno.
All the traffic noise and bustle and scents of Florence
came rising up on the balmy evening air, and Jess
breathed in deeply, savouring it as she craned her neck
to get a glimpse of the Ponte Vecchio in the distance.

''Fantastic,'' she said, going inside. ''Shall I leave the
doors open?''

''Yes, please.'' Emily smiled ruefully. ''At last I can
listen to Florence, even though I can't explore the city
just yet. Hurry up, Jess. I want a blow-by-blow description of the wedding.''

Jess showered quickly, dried her hair and brushed it into shape, then curled up on the other bed and settled down to take Emily through the wedding day from start to finish. "I know brides are supposed to look beautiful, but you needed sunglasses just to look at Leo. Jonah couldn't take his eyes off her. Neither," she added ruefully, "could Roberto Forli."

"I'm amazed he was there!"

"So was I—but I'm very glad he was, because in the end it meant Lorenzo came to the wedding, too." Jess was silent for a moment. "Do you realise, Em," she said at last, "that this time last week I'd never even heard of Lorenzo Forli, let alone set eyes on him? And now—"

"And now?"

"I feel as though I've known him for ever." Jess leapt off the bed. "Right. Enough of me. Let's think about you. What are you having for supper?"

When a tempting herb omelette arrived Emily managed to eat some of it, under her friend's watchful eye, but asked for mercy eventually, and Jess removed the tray and plumped up the pillows.

"I'll help you tidy up, shall I?"

"If you like. Do I look so awful, then?"

"No. But Lorenzo's coming to meet you before he takes me to dinner."

This piece of news threw the invalid into a panic. She demanded help to the bathroom, managed to wash her own face afterwards, then brushed her own hair while Jess remade the bed.

"Right then, Em. In you go."

When Emily was sitting up against the pillows with her new book she flapped a hand at Jess. "Shoo! Go and gild the lily. It's you Lorenzo wants, not me."

A little before eight Jess was ready, in a sleeveless,

V-necked jersey dress, the lustrous bitter chocolate shade a perfect match for eyes which gleamed with anticipation beneath the gleaming fall of hair across her forehead.

"Yummy," said Emily as Jess gave a pirouette. "Like a gorgeous hand-made chocolate. Lorenzo will take one look and want to gobble you up." She grinned as a knock on the door silenced Jess's protests. "Go on. Let him in."

When Jess opened the door Lorenzo gave her an all-encompassing scrutiny, then kissed his fingers to her in reverent silence. She mimed a kiss in return, then ushered him into the room and introduced him to Emily.

*"Piacere."* Lorenzo smiled gently and took the hand the invalid held out, retaining it in his for a moment. "How are you feeling, Miss Shaw?"

"Emily, please!" She returned the smile shyly. "I can hardly help but feel better after all you've done for me, Mr—"

"Lorenzo, *per favore,*" he corrected quickly. "I am here not only for the pleasure of meeting you, but to make sure there is nothing you need."

"You've thought of everything," she assured him. "I can't tell you how grateful I am. I wish there was some way I could repay you."

"That is easy. You have only to make a full recovery," he assured her. "Jessamy has told you I am driving you to my home tomorrow?"

Emily went very pink. "Yes, indeed. It's amazingly kind of you."

"Lorenzo, how do you think she looks?" said Jess later, as they walked towards the lift.

"Very fragile, *cara.* But do not worry. I have asked Anna to accompany us for a few days to look after her."

"This is all a huge expense for you," said Jess, frowning.

"I am being selfish. I do not wish you to tire yourself with constant nursing." Lorenzo shrugged. "I promise you I can afford professional medical care for a few days. Otherwise where is the problem? You will be living in my house, with my cook preparing your meals. But none of that matters," he added, as they entered the lift. "As I have said before, *carissima*, for you I would do anything."

Jess reached up to touch a caressing hand to his cheek, her eyes narrowing suddenly as it dawned on her that the lift was going up, instead of down. "Do you have two restaurants in the hotel, then?"

"No. One only." When the lift stopped at the top floor Jess gave him a questioning look as she stepped out into a corridor with arched windows which gave it the look of a colonnade. Lorenzo led her towards a pair of double doors at the end, unlocked them and gave her a little bow as he led her through a small foyer, and opened one of the doors to usher her into what was very obviously the salon of a private apartment.

Jess stood very still just inside a large, beautiful room which opened out onto a balcony. The furniture was elegant: chairs and sofas upholstered in velvet and brocade, paintings and mirrors in carved, gilded frames on the walls. And in eye-catching prominence in the centre of the room a small table was laid for two, complete with a silver vase of flowers. She eyed it all with dismay, only now realising how much she'd wanted to dine in the hotel restaurant, with Lorenzo attentive at her side, displaying pride in his companion to the world. His world.

"The apartment you spoke of," said Jess tonelessly at

last. "I assumed it was somewhere else in the city. But I was wrong, wasn't I? You live here, in the hotel."

Lorenzo frowned. "Yes. Of course. What is wrong, Jessamy? I thought you would prefer to dine alone with me here. Downstairs in the restaurant all my staff would naturally take much interest in my—my companion."

"Instead," she said lightly, "they'll think you've brought me here for a lot more than just dinner. This, I assume, is where you bring the ladies who allow those privileges you talked about."

The animation drained from Lorenzo's face, leaving it blank as a Venetian carnival mask. "I bring no one here except family," he said, after a long, painful interval. "This is my private place." He strode past her towards a telephone on the carved credenza. "Like a fool I thought you would be happier here than in the public restaurant. That you would want to be alone with me." He shrugged negligently. "No matter. I shall ring to reserve a table."

"Not much point in that," said Jess, disappointment sharpening her voice. "The damage is done."

"The only damage is to my pride," he retorted with arrogance. "No one knows the identity of my guest, Jessamy. However, since you so obviously do not wish to dine with me after all, I shall ask for a table for one in the restaurant. You may eat there alone."

Jess stared at him in utter dismay. "I can't do that."

"Then I shall escort you back to your friend, and you shall ring for room service." His eyes glittered coldly, and Jess shivered, appalled at the sudden chasm yawning between them. One unconsidered step, she realised in sudden panic, could plunge her into it, with no way out. And belatedly she remembered how much she was indebted to him.

"I'm sorry," she said in a constricted voice quite unlike her own. "I didn't mean to offend you. Especially after you've been so kind—"

"Do not insult me by talking of expense again," he flung at her.

"Lorenzo, please," she said in desperation. "If I've jumped to the wrong conclusion I apologise."

He stared at her malevolently. "You thought I brought you here to rush you straight into my bed, it seems. Perhaps even before I allowed you to eat dinner."

"Like Lord Byron—" Jess bit her lip, cursing, not for the first time, her tendency to say the first thing that came into her head when she was nervous.

Lorenzo looked blank. "*Mi scusi?* What is your poet to do with this?" The cold glitter faded from his eyes as they followed the tide of colour which rose from the neckline of her dress to the roots of her hair.

"I read a book about him once. A biography," she said gruffly, unable to look at him. "On his wedding day he—he disposed of his wife's virginity on the sofa before dinner."

Lorenzo breathed in so deeply she could tell, even without looking at him, that he was fighting to master his temper. "And when you saw this room you expected me to do the same?"

"No. Not exactly." Jess raised her head and looked him in the eye. "That wouldn't have been possible."

Without taking his eyes from hers he gestured towards a deep-cushioned couch upholstered in honey-coloured velvet. "I have a sofa," he said very quietly.

Jess nodded. "But I'm not a virgin."

# CHAPTER SEVEN

THE WORDS echoed in the room, and, suddenly desperate for air, Jess turned on her heel and went out onto the balcony. By this time the moon was high enough to paint a glittering path across the Arno. She leaned her hands on the balcony rail to gaze down at it blindly, cursing herself for a fool. She was twenty-four years old, without a shred of false modesty about her appeal to men. No one in the world she came from would expect her to be inexperienced. Yet she been mad enough to fling the fact in Lorenzo's face like a gauntlet because she wanted him to know before... Before she became his lover, of course. And if that was her intention, *and* her desire, as she now so clearly saw it was, it seemed a touch irrational to make a fuss about dining alone with him in his apartment.

Slim brown hands appeared beside hers to grasp the balcony rail.

Jess stood very still, conscious in every nerve of the male presence beside her. She glanced up at last at the dauntingly stern profile. "Lorenzo, I'm sorry. I've behaved like an idiot. But it was something Emily said just before you came for me."

He looked down at her, frowning. "Emily? What did she say?"

"When I was ready she said I looked—"

"*Incantevole?*"

"What does that mean?"

"Ravishing," he informed her, something in his voice

telling her that hostilities, if not over, were at least suspended.

"She actually said you'd want to gobble me up," Jess muttered.

"What is this 'gobble'?" he demanded.

"Devour, I suppose."

"Ah!" Lorenzo nodded. "I see. And when I brought you here you assumed she was right."

Jess slanted a troubled look at him. "I wouldn't blame you. From the night we met I've given you every reason to believe that the moment the opportunity arose I would share your bed. I won't lie. I want this, too. Some time soon."

"But not as soon as this."

"Exactly. Which is why I was upset and nervous and started babbling about Byron."

"Unlike the poet, I would have given you dinner first, I swear," he assured her, and took her hand. When she curled her fingers round his in relief he gave her a very direct look. "You are a woman of much allure, Jessamy. I did not imagine for one moment that you were a virgin. Why did you feel you had to tell me that?"

She stared down at their clasped hands. "I suppose because you said there should be truth between us. And after that nonsense about Byron it just came out. I thought that maybe here, in Italy, even someone my age might be expected—"

"To be a virgin," he finished for her.

"Right. And after your experience with Renata I wanted you to know this first. Not—" She halted, her face hot again.

"Not during the rapture of our first night together," he said, a deepened note in his voice which sent a great shiver down her spine. "You are cold," he said instantly, but she shook her head.

"No. Not in the least." She looked at him in appeal. "As I've told you before, it's the effect you have on me. Would you put your arms around me, Lorenzo? Please?"

His eyes dilated, his fingers suddenly cruelly tight on hers. "Come inside, then. Out here I feel as if the eyes of the world are on us."

Once inside the beautiful, formal room he dropped her hand, removed his jacket, then stood very still, just looking at her, and after a moment or two Jess realised it was up to her to make the first move. She went to him, arms outstretched, and with a smile which made her bones feel hollow Lorenzo drew her close against him, bending his dark head to hers. She could felt his heart thudding against hers, and clutching him closer so that he could kiss her and make everything better. The kiss made everything so much better that in a very short time both of them were ravenous for more than mere food. Then Jess's stomach gave a great, unromantic grumble and Lorenzo put her away from him, laughing uproariously.

"You are hungry!"

She nodded, giggling like a schoolgirl. "Yes. I am. Now."

He raised a quizzical eyebrow. "Now?"

"I couldn't have eaten a thing a while ago, when you were angry with me."

He grasped her by the shoulders and shook her gently. "You were angry with me, also, Jessamy."

She bit her lip. "I've said I'm sorry."

"I need more than words to heal my hurt!"

Jess reached up to wind her arms round his neck and kissed him with such passionate contrition Lorenzo put her away at last, breathing hard.

"We must eat," he said unsteadily. "Before you tempt me into behaving like your mad, bad Byron. But first," he added with sudden emphasis, "my only reason for bringing you here tonight was something you said during the flight."

She eyed him in surprise. "What did I say?"

"You said you would prefer me to kiss you in private, Jessamy. So. Instead of showing you off in triumph in the restaurant I chose to bring you here." His eyes held hers. "But only to kiss, and to touch, perhaps. Nothing more. You believe this?"

"Yes," said Jess in deep remorse. "Of course I do."

Lorenzo seated her with much ceremony at the table. "Our dinner is in the refrigerator in my seldom-used kitchen. For this, our first meal together, I chose dishes which would wait as long as we wished. So tonight I must play waiter." He went from the room, then returned with a tray he placed on the credenza. He set two plates on the table, then opened the bottle of wine, his eyes dancing. "And tonight we shall actually drink some prosecco, no?"

"Yes!" Jess smiled radiantly as he filled her glass.

He sat down, gazing into her eyes. "What shall we drink to?"

She thought for a moment, then raised her glass. "To truth—always!"

*"Sempre la verità,"* he echoed.

The meal would have been tempting if Jess had possessed no appetite at all. As it was, with their first quarrel behind them, her relief was intense at surviving it without alienating Lorenzo for ever. Suddenly hungry, she was quick to start on the salad of San Daniele ham and figs, and savoured the flavours of mint and basil with enthusiasm Lorenzo viewed with open approval.

"At last, I see you eat," he said with satisfaction.

"I do it all the time—too much, sometimes," she assured him indistinctly. "Which is why I'm never going to be like Leo or Kate."

"Why should you wish to be?" he said, frowning.

"They can eat anything they like and stay slim." She smiled at him philosophically. "I tend to get a bit too rounded if I indulge too often."

"Rounded," he repeated, lingering on the word with pleasure. "I like this very much. I prefer a woman who curves in and out in certain delectable places. Like you, *amore*."

So she was *amore* again. Euphoric with relief, Jess began with enthusiasm on the main course of filleted salmon served with anchovy and caper mayonnaise, and sat back at last with a blissful sigh. "That was perfect," she informed him, and got up to take their plates, waving Lorenzo back when he would have done it for her. "No, let me. I need to make up to you for being so horrible." She shook her head. "When I think of all you've done—"

"Please! I do not wish to hear this." He paused, eyeing her intently. "Jessamy, when I spoke of my reward on the plane, did you really think I meant to claim this tonight? In payment for an air fare and a few medical bills for your friend?"

"*No!* That never occurred to me. But when you brought me here and I saw the scene set like this—" She shrugged ruefully. "I was afraid that history was repeating itself."

Lorenzo's eyes narrowed. "What is this history, Jessamy?"

"Are you sure you want to hear? The story of my love-life is short enough, goodness knows, but *very* boring."

"Not to me," he assured her. "Nothing about you could bore me. Tell me. Start at the very beginning of this love-life of yours. The very first man in your life."

Jess sat down and put out a hand and Lorenzo grasped it, smiling in encouragement. "Very well, then," she began, resigned. "I experienced my first run-in with sex— it certainly wasn't love—with the boy who took me home from the farewell dance at my school. I was seventeen."

Lorenzo's grasp tightened. "He was also young?"

Jess nodded. "But older than me. In more ways than one. He was captain of games at his own school, and good-looking in a hunky kind of way."

"Hunky?"

"More muscles and hormones than brains."

"Ah." Lorenzo nodded, enlightened.

"I'd had such a good time. Mother bought me a great dress, Leo did my hair, and all my friends envied me my partner because he was the best-looking boy there. He drove me home in the moonlight in his father's car, and on the way back he parked in a lane, took a rug from the back seat and suggested a stroll down to the river. I thought he just wanted a few kisses. Which he did, to start with. But he'd come prepared for a lot more than that. In every way." She pulled a face. "He was a big, muscular lad and very fit. I didn't stand a chance."

Lorenzo frowned darkly. "He hurt you?"

"He certainly did. I fought like a wildcat, which was not only useless and gave me bruises, but excited him so much that when he got his way at last it was over almost as soon as it had begun. He was furious and humiliated, I was hysterical with rage, and he drove me home at such speed it's a wonder we both got there in one piece. I never heard from him again. Nor," she added, eyes flashing, "did I want to."

Lorenzo said something short and expressive in his own tongue, then raised her hand to his lips, eyeing her questioningly. "And this came back to haunt you tonight?"

"Heavens, no!" Jess drank some of her wine. "I just mentioned it to explain my reluctance to repeat the experience. It would be different, I told myself, when I actually fell in love. I just had to wait until that happy day arrived." She shook her head sadly. "One day I really thought it had. But when we got as far as bed at last the whole thing left me cold. So the man vanished into the night in a huff."

"Were you heartbroken?" asked Lorenzo tenderly.

"Not in the slightest." Jess pulled a face. "In fact, I was beginning to wonder if I really *had* a heart. Emily falls in and out of love with amazing regularity, but I prefer men who just want to be friends."

"Do you know many men like that?" he asked, astonished.

"Not many, no. But eventually, quite a long time after fiasco number two, I met a man who'd just survived a divorce, and he agreed that platonic relationships were less trouble than the other kind."

"Ah!" A smile played at the corners of Lorenzo's mouth. "But he failed to keep to this, of course?"

"Right. He got in the habit of inviting me to his new flat to watch a video, order in Chinese, that kind of thing. But one night I arrived to find a table set for two, with champagne, candles, even red roses. You can guess the rest. The champagne didn't work. Nothing worked. At least not for me." Her eyes darkened. "He became quite objectionable, so this time *I* went off in a huff."

Lorenzo nodded slowly. "Now I understand your feelings when I brought you here tonight."

Jess smiled. Lorenzo's apartment was a far cry from the London flat she'd stormed out of in such a rage. "My disappointment tonight," she said with precision, "was for a quite different reason."

"Tell me this reason," he commanded.

"It's hard to put into words."

"Try!"

"I was really looking forward to eating in the hotel dining room with you," she admitted, flushing. "I liked the idea of everyone looking at us and knowing that you, that I—" She halted, her eyes locked with his.

"That you were mine?" he said softly.

Jess went pale, her dark, startled eyes wide as they stared into his. "Is that how you think of me?"

"Yes," he said simply. "Since the moment I first saw you I feel this. There is no way to explain it—"

"Wise men never try," she said huskily.

There was a sudden, charged silence between them.

"This is dangerous," said Lorenzo abruptly. "You were right. We should have dined in the restaurant."

"I'm glad now that we didn't," she assured him.

"Why?" he demanded.

"Because we couldn't have talked like this. Nor," she added, looking him in the eye, "could you have kissed me, touched me, just as you said you wanted."

Lorenzo tensed, like a panther about to spring, and for a moment Jess was sure he would pull her out of her chair and kiss her senseless. Instead, to her intense disappointment, he fetched a plate from the credenza and set it in front of her. "This is a *torta*, made of almonds and lemon and ricotta," he said, the uneven huskiness of his voice at odds with the prosaic words. "Is this to your taste?"

Jess stared at the confection blankly. "Normally, yes.

But not right now. Perhaps I could take it down to Emily later. She loves this kind of thing. Do have some yourself, of course.''

"No," he said explosively. "You know very well that it is not cake that I want." His eyes lit with a heat which dried her mouth. "I cannot forget that tonight, Jessamy, may be the only time we can be together like this. At the Villa Fortuna it will be difficult for me."

Jess stiffened. Was there some sinister reason why he wouldn't want to make love to her at the villa? Suddenly the reason hit her like a punch in the stomach.

"What is it?" he demanded, and at last pulled her up out of her chair. "Tell me! Why do you look like that?"

"I never thought to ask," she said in a rush. "Is the Villa Fortuna the home you shared with Renata?"

"Ah, no, *carssima*, it is not!" he assured her, and held her close for a moment, then led her across the room to a deep, comfortable sofa and drew her down beside him.

"I should have made this clear before, Jessamy. When Renata died I sold the house we lived in. The Villa Fortuna is my family home, where I grew up with Roberto and my sister."

"I didn't know you had a sister." Jess let out a deep sigh and relaxed against him, limp with relief. The prospect of staying in a house haunted by the ghost of Lorenzo's wife was the stuff of nightmares. "What's your sister's name? Where does she live? Is she married?"

He laughed and kissed the top of her head. "Isabella is younger than Roberto. She is married to a lawyer called Andrea Moretti. They have two small sons and live in Lucca." He turned her face to his. "*Allora*, you feel better?"

"Yes. Much better. Where *did* you live, Lorenzo?"

"Renata's parents wanted us to make our home with them, but to hide the truth of our marriage it was necessary for us to live alone. I bought a house far away from them, in Oltrano, over there." He gestured towards the balcony, his eyes sombre. "It became a prison for both of us."

"Is that why you wanted to come inside just now? Because you can't bear to look over there?"

"No!" His arm tightened. "It was solely a burning desire for privacy with you, *amore*."

Deeply gratified, Jess leaned up to kiss his cheek. "Poor Renata. Though in some ways I think she was very fortunate."

*"Fortunate?"*

"To be married to you, Lorenzo. Other men, in the same circumstances, might not have been so forbearing."

He shook his head. "Do not endow me with virtues I lack, Jessamy."

"What do you mean?"

"I was forbearing, as you say, because I had no desire to be otherwise. Something died inside me the night Renata rejected me. My youth, perhaps," he added, with a twist to his mouth. "After that night, unless we were in public and it was unavoidable, I never touched her again." Lorenzo put a finger under her chin and raised her face to his. When I met you, *amore*, feelings I thought were dead for ever came to life, as though a dam had burst and all the suppressed longings of those empty years came rushing through." He smiled wryly into her startled eyes. "I am being very Italian and emotional, am I not? Does it embarrass you, *piccola*?"

"Not in the least," she assured him. To be called 'little one' in that husky, caressing voice ignited several emotions inside Jess, but not one of them was embarrassment.

"If you want the truth, I just love it when you get all Latin and passionate. It thrills me to bits—"

Lorenzo smothered the rest of her words with his mouth, and she responded with such ardour it was a long time before there was any more conversation. And when Lorenzo began to speak at last they were words Jess understood only by their intonation as he made love to her in his own tongue, the liquid flow of musical endearments as seductive as the slim, sure hands that moved over her in light, delicate caresses which, even through the clinging silk of her dress, sent fiery streaks of longing to a secret place which throbbed in unaccustomed response.

After only minutes of the delicate torture Jess longed for Lorenzo to undress her, and carry her to his bed and show her, at last, just how wonderful the act of love could be. But she knew he wasn't going to do that. At least, not tonight. Assailed by emotions and physical longings unfamiliar to her, she began to cry, and Lorenzo crushed her close in remorse.

"Do not weep, *amore*. Forgive me—I have frightened you."

"No, you haven't," she said thickly. "I'm not frightened, I'm *frustrated*. I—I long for you, Lorenzo. You're driving me crazy. I've never felt like this before."

He groaned. "Do not say such things to me, *carissima*." He held her face in his hands, his eyes questioning as they met the look in hers. "What is it?"

"You said that it would be difficult to be alone together at the Villa Fortuna. Is this because of Emily, and the nurse?"

Lorenzo nodded, resigned. "Also there is Carla, who cooks for me, and Mario, her husband, who takes care of the property, and the moment Isabella learns I have guests, she will come rushing to meet you."

Jess bit her lip. "Won't your sister find it odd? That you've invited me to stay at your house?"

Lorenzo sat in silence for some time, his eyes fixed on their entwined hands. "She will be very surprised," he said at last, his voice deeper and more uneven than it had been. "Because I have never invited a woman there before." He looked up again, his eyes alight with an urgency which took her breath away. "I did not mean to say this. At least, not tonight. I told myself I must wait, be patient. But, *Dio*, I have wasted enough of my life already." His grasp tightened. "I knew from the first moment I saw you that I wanted you for my own. Not for a *relazione*—a love affair—but for ever. I want you for my wife, Jessamy."

## CHAPTER EIGHT

JESS sat very still, gazing at him in silence broken only by the night-time sounds of Florence coming through the open balcony doors. A voice in her head suggested, without much hope, that this was too sudden, too soon, but her turbulent heart brushed it aside, clamouring that this was what she'd been waiting for all her adult life.

"It is too soon," said Lorenzo bitterly, and thrust a hand through his thick black hair. "I am a fool. I should have waited—"

"No," said Jess swiftly. She gave him a smile so incandescent his eyes blazed in response. "I'm glad you couldn't wait."

He seized her hands in a grasp which threatened to crack her bones. "You mean this?"

"Yes."

"You are saying you will marry me, Jessamy?"

*"Yes."*

"Then tell me that you love me!"

"Of course I love you," she said unevenly. "Otherwise we wouldn't be having this conversation."

Lorenzo leapt to his feet, pulling her with him, his face stern as he gazed down into hers. "You realise that the world will say you have known me too short a time to be sure of your feelings."

"Do you care?" she demanded.

He cupped her face in his hands. "I care only for you. And for what your parents will think. We must talk to them—"

"Not yet," Jess said hastily. "I don't want to tell anyone yet."

"Not even your friend?"

"Emily knows already," Jess assured him, then laughed at his look of astonished delight. "That I love you, I mean. I've never been madly in love before—I had to tell someone!"

*"Meraviglioso!"* His eyes lit with a triumphant gleam. "If your friend knows this life will be easier at the Villa Fortuna than I thought. She will expect us to want time alone together, no?"

"She will, yes," agreed Jess, and smiled at him expectantly. "I don't know how you do things in Italy, darling, but in my part of the world it's the custom to exchange a kiss once a proposal is accepted."

Lorenzo's eyes kindled. "Say 'darling' again!"

"Kiss me first."

Lorenzo picked her up instead, and for a wild moment Jess wondered if he meant to carry her straight to bed now their relationship had altered. Instead he sank down with her on the sofa, settling her in his lap as he kissed the mouth she held up in invitation.

"Now, *amore*," he breathed against her parted lips, "it is I who cannot believe this is real."

"If it's a dream, we're sharing it," she whispered, and responded with uninhibited delight to the mouth which showed her that mere kissing itself was an art form in which Lorenzo Forli possessed so much skill that Jess pulled away a little at last, smiling in challenge.

"Who taught you to kiss like that?" she demanded breathlessly.

He laughed, and ruffled the bright hair falling over her forehead. "Francesca."

"Who was *she*?" demanded Jess, sitting up.

Lorenzo pulled her back down against his shoulder. "Just a girl I knew when I was young, long before my marriage. She was older than me, and taught me that kisses and caresses are as important as the act of love itself. Not," he added with regret, "that Francesca ever allowed me more than the kisses, you understand."

"But you wanted more!"

His sudden grin stripped years from him. "Men always want more, *tesoro*." He breathed in deeply. "Now we must be practical. I am asking a great deal of you—I know this. Are you really willing to give up your career to share my life here with me, Jessamy?"

She hesitated, then nodded. "Yes, I am."

"You have doubts?" he asked quietly.

"No. None. In fact—" Jess smiled a little, then shrugged. "This is something I've never admitted to another soul. My so-called career has never really been important to me at all. I just pretended it was."

Lorenzo frowned. "But why should you need to pretend, *carissima*?"

"I had to have something special in my life. I'm not brainless, nor am I lazy, but I'm not in the least academic, like the rest of my family. Leo got a good degree, and I'm sure Adam has done well in Edinburgh, too, while Kate will do brilliantly, probably better than either of them." She smiled wryly. "I'm the odd one out, even to the straight hair—"

"Your hair is beautiful," he contradicted, and smoothed it back from her forehead. "And it will be even more beautiful when it grows longer, Jessamy," he added slyly, then kissed the mouth she opened to protest. "Go on," he said unevenly. "I am listening, *carissima*."

Jess took a deep breath. "After school I did a course which made me computer-literate, and I got a job in advertising, making it clear to all concerned that I was intent on a career. Eventually I worked for one of the men I told you about.'' She sighed. ''This meant that when the relationship went wrong I was forced to resign. So much for my advertising career. My present job is interesting, and I enjoy it.'' Jess looked at him squarely. ''But to be honest I hate the thought of doing it for the rest of my working life.''

Lorenzo pulled her closer, his eyes gleaming with relief. ''I am delighted to hear this. Also very happy that your career in London will not come between us.''

''May be I could do something here in Florence, or—'' She halted.

''Or?'' he prompted.

''Or perhaps we'll have a baby right away.'' Jess kept her eyes on the brown muscular throat visible through the open collar of Lorenzo's shirt, and saw it grow taut in response to her words.

''You mean this, *amore*?'' he demanded incredulously. ''You would like a baby?''

''Not *a* baby,'' she corrected breathlessly. ''*Your* baby.''

He crushed her close, his English deserting him as he unleashed a flood of passionate Italian which flowed over Jess in a torrent of feeling which left her in no doubt as to his reaction.

''I had given up all hope of children of my own,'' he said at last in English, his voice rough with emotion.

''But surely you must have met women who would have been only too delighted to give you babies?'' said Jess.

Lorenzo gave a very Latin shrug. ''Perhaps. But I swore never to marry again without love. Once,'' he added grimly, ''was enough.''

Jess pulled his head down to hers, experiencing a great urge to comfort him any way she could. She kissed him passionately, her arms locked round his neck, telling him without words how much she cared, feeling his heart thudding against hers as he whispered a great many things she knew would be gratifying if she could only understand them.

"I will teach you Italian," he said in between kisses. "I cannot make love in English."

"You're doing brilliantly," she gasped.

"I can do much better—"

There was sudden silence between them. They gazed at each other, both pairs of eyes dilated with shared desire.

Lorenzo jumped to his feet, pulling her with him. "I must take you back to your friend."

"It's early," objected Jess.

"No matter." He stared down at her wildly. "I want you so much, *amore*, you know this. I feel such fire, such longing to possess, I have no—no confidence in my power to—*Dio!*" he added in frustration. "I cannot find the words." He drew in a deep, steadying breath. "Jessamy, I swear that my intention was not the same as those other men. The meal, the wine, they were merely food and drink, not a means to lure you to my bed."

"I know that now," she said disconsolately, and laid her head against his shoulder. "Lorenzo."

"*Si?*"

"Are you saying you're not going to make love to me until we're married?"

"If that is your wish, most certainly."

She put her arms round his lean waist and tipped her face back, shaking her head. "It's not. I want you to make love to me before then. Even—even if it's not perfect between us at first."

"You confuse me with your other lovers!" he said arrogantly, and smiled. "We were meant for each other, Jessamy. How could it not be perfect?"

"It might not be. But that isn't important. I meant that by our wedding night I wanted it to *be* perfect," she said urgently, and saw comprehension blaze in his eyes.

"To erase bad memories? Ah, Jessamy. *Amore.* I am so right to think of you as my reward." Lorenzo kissed her with fierce tenderness, then drew away a little to smile into her eyes. "Now you have consented to be mine," he whispered, "very soon I shall show you just what love can be. But in the meantime—"

"You're going to take me back to Emily," she said, resigned.

He shook his head and drew her down to the deep velvet couch again. "Not yet. Anna can look after your friend for at least another hour. This is a very special moment in our lives, *innamorata*. I need to hold you in my arms for a while."

Lorenzo began to kiss her, gently at first, with subtle kisses which moved over her eyelids and cheeks and along her jaw before coming to rest on her waiting mouth. Her lips parted eagerly, her tongue meeting his with an ardour which hurried Lorenzo's breathing. He laid her back against the velvet cushions and hung over her, looking down into her face as though watchful for any look of dissent as his hands sought her breasts, smoothing and stroking through the thin, clinging fabric. Jess gazed back, mesmerised, stirring restlessly beneath caresses she could only just bear. Then the long, skilful fingers slid beneath the neckline of her dress, and his touch on her erect, sensitive nipples took her breath away.

Lorenzo kissed her deeply, drawing her down to lie full length against him, and Jess felt heat flood through her as she came into contact with his arousal. Feeling him hard and throbbing with explicit promise ignited something wild and new inside her, and she pulled away to reach behind her back, tugging down the zip of her dress to let it slide from her shoulders. Lorenzo breathed in sharply, pushed scraps of flesh-coloured silk aside and bent his head to her breasts, his mouth hot against her skin as he captured a diamond-hard nipple between his lips. Jess shook from head to foot as his lips, teeth and subtle, expert fingers swiftly roused her to a fever-pitch of need. She thrust her hands into his thick black hair to clutch him closer still, but after a moment or two Lorenzo sat up to strip off his shirt and crush her against his bare chest, kissing her mouth with a frenzied hunger she met with equal fire.

At long last Lorenzo lifted his dark, dishevelled head to look in her eyes. *"Innamorata,"* he said hoarsely.

"I want you so much, Lorenzo," she gasped.

"I want you more!" He closed his eyes in anguish for a moment, then leapt up, reaching for his shirt.

Jess got to her feet, and turned her back on him to reach for her zip, silent tears sliding down her cheeks as she struggled to do up her dress.

"Let me!" Lorenzo put her hands aside gently, then stiffened and spun her round in his arms. "You are crying," he accused.

"No, I'm not," she croaked, and sniffed inelegantly.

"It is no sin to cry," he assured her, and bent to kiss the tears away. The fleeting contact was too much for either of them. In an instant their arms were straining each other close as their lips met in an engulfing kiss which vanquished any last shred of control either of them possessed. Lorenzo picked her up, his eyes wild and questioning on hers, and Jess gave him a look of such smouldering invitation he carried her from the room and set her on her feet at last beside a wide bed bathed in moonlight.

"You are sure?" he demanded hoarsely.

"Utterly sure," she whispered, and shrugged the dress from her shoulders, stepping out of it as it slithered to the floor.

Lorenzo sank to his knees before her, burying his face against the satiny skin of her waist. "I love you so much—I burn for you. I am not sure I can be gentle."

"I don't *want* you to be gentle," she said fiercely. "I just need to know."

He raised his head. "To know?"

"That I'm not frigid, or abnormal, or any of those things I've been accused of in the past—" She gasped as in one lithe movement Lorenzo leapt to his feet, swept her up in his arms and laid her on the bed.

He hung over her, his eyes blazing darkly in a face rendered pale as marble by the bleaching moonlight. "They were fools! You are perfect."

Tears slid from the corners of her eyes again. "Darling, I wish—"

"What is it you wish, *amore*?"

"That there had never been anyone else."

"Forget the past!" Lorenzo licked the tears away. "You and I," he promised huskily, "will find rapture together."

And when the final barriers of clothes were gone and they lay naked in each other's arms all memory of things past was blotted out for both of them as Lorenzo kissed and caressed her into hunger as great as his own. Jess shivered and gasped as his lips and hands wrought magic so overwhelming that she could bear it no longer. She uttered a hoarse, desperate little plea and Lorenzo thrust home to make their union complete. For a moment he lay tense and still, controlling his urgency, but Jess moved in urgent invitation, and Lorenzo responded with delight, increasing the rhythm by subtle degrees, kissing and caressing her and telling her how exquisite, how beautiful she felt in his arms, before his English deserted him and he resorted to liquid Italian endearments as he took her along the path to their mutual goal. Her eyes dilated and her breathing grew ragged, and her head began to toss back and forth on the pillow. At last Jess dug desperate, demanding fingers into his shoulders, and they surged together in hot, throbbing turbulence which mounted to a final paroxysm of pulsating sensation she experienced seconds before Lorenzo let out a great gasp and surrendered to the release he'd denied himself until he felt her convulse in the ultimate pleasure beneath him.

They lay in each other's arms for a long time before Lorenzo, with deep reluctance, stirred at last. He raised his head to smile into her heavy eyes.

"So, *mi amore*, tell me how you feel."

Jess considered it gravely. "Triumphant," she decided at last.

He let out a deep, relishing sigh, and rubbed his cheek against hers. "So you will not go away in this huff of yours?"

"No, indeed. I'm not sure I can even move."

"I do not wish you to move! But it is time I returned you to your friend."

"I wish I could stay."

He kissed her swiftly. "When we are married I shall hold you in my arms all night."

Jess stretched happily at the thought, then winced.

"What is it?" he said in alarm.

"A good thing you can't see me properly," she said gruffly. "I'm blushing."

He laughed and held her close. "Why?"

"Certain muscles unused to such activity are protesting," she said ruefully, then raised a hand to touch his cheek. "Thank you, Lorenzo. For making such magic for me."

"*You* are thanking *me*?" he said incredulously. "It was so beautiful, Jessamy, to feel your body so responsive to mine. When I brought you here tonight I did not expect such rapture."

"Before I met you I never expected it at all. Ever." Jess smiled at him radiantly, and he held her close, rubbing his cheek against hers until she asked for mercy.

"*Scusi!*" he said penitently. "When we are married I promise I shall shave every night before we go to bed."

The intimacy of this struck Jess with such force she breathed in sharply. "I still can't believe this is happening, darling."

Lorenzo nodded vigorously. "I know, *piccola*. I feel this also." He raised himself on an elbow to look down at her. "Believe that I love you, Jessamy Dysart," he said very quietly.

"I do." Jess returned the look very steadily. "I love you too, Lorenzo Forli."

And as though they'd exchanged a vow, Lorenzo picked up her hand and kissed the finger which would wear his ring. "Come, *carissima*. It is time to go."

Jess heaved a sigh. "If we must. But first I need to tidy up."

After an interval spent in Lorenzo's bathroom Jess presented herself for inspection in the soft lamplight of the beautiful outer room.

"Do I look all right?" she asked anxiously.

He smiled appreciatively. "Good enough to gobble up, as your friend would say."

"Lorenzo," said Jess suddenly. "There's something you should know."

His smile faded. "Tell me, then."

Her eyes fell. "I don't count the fiasco with the schoolboy, but I'd known the other two a long time before—"

"Before you became lovers?"

She nodded, flushing as she slid her feet into the famous sandals. "I wouldn't describe the arrangement like that, but that's what I meant, yes."

Lorenzo took her hands in his, looking down at her very soberly. "You are telling me that it is not your habit to make love with a man you've known such a short time. But for you and for me it is different. I love you, Jessamy."

"I love you, too," she said, oddly shy now.

"I asked you to marry me. And you consented. A church ceremony will make no difference to the way I feel," he assured her. "To me you are already my wife."

Jess felt tears well up in her eyes, and smiled at him damply. "Sorry. I'm not usually the weepy kind."

"Do not apologise, *carissima*, I love to kiss your tears away—"

"Remember what happened last time," she reminded him, sniffing hard.

He heaved in a deep sigh. "I do. Most vividly. So come. Let us go before I scandalise Anna by returning you after midnight."

"Hold me for a moment," she said gruffly.

"For the rest of my life!" he assured her, and held her up against him so that she stood on tiptoe and had to wreath her arms round his waist to keep her balance.

"I need your arms around me to convince myself this is all happening," she whispered.

Lorenzo looked deep into her eyes. "This is no fairy-tale, *Cenerentola*, this is real life. Our life." His arms tightened. "Now you have given yourself to me you are mine. I shall never let you go."

# CHAPTER NINE

EMILY was too sleepy to do more than ask if Jess had enjoyed herself, and once Anna had gone to the room Lorenzo had reserved for her, Jess showered swiftly and slid into bed, reliving the evening over and over again before she slept at last. She woke only when the nurse arrived early next morning to see to Emily, which ruled out any private conversation with her friend, and Jess was grateful for it. The magic with Lorenzo was a glorious, private secret. And in the bright light of morning, despite Lorenzo's parting words, it was still hard to believe that the whole episode wasn't some figment of her imagination.

When her last relationship had soured Jess had been philosophical when Leonie questioned her about it. "Some day my prince will come," she'd said flippantly, but had never really expected a fairy tale scenario for herself. Ever. Yet now, with Lorenzo, it seemed that the dreams she'd once dreamed had finally come true.

While she shared an early breakfast with a slightly improved Emily, Jess described the delicious dinner she'd eaten, but because Anna was bustling about, preparing for the journey to the Villa Fortuna, she made no mention of dining alone with Lorenzo in his private apartment.

"I'm entitled to loss of appetite, but you're not," Emily accused, when Jess contented herself with orange juice and coffee.

"You know I never eat breakfast!"

Emily cast a knowing eye on her friend's dreaming face and raised an expressive eyebrow, Anna's presence preventing any teasing.

Due to Anna's efficiency Emily was bathed and dressed and ready well before time, but looked even less robust once she was on her feet.

"Take it easy, Em," said Jess, sitting her down in a chair near the open balcony doors. "Apparently it's not far to the villa, and when we get there you can go straight to bed, if you want."

"It is most necessary that she does so after the journey," said Anna firmly. "Dottore Tosti orders this. Tomorrow, Emily, you shall get up for a longer time."

"Yes, Nurse," said the invalid, so meekly it was plain that the thought of bed was more welcome than Emily cared to let on.

A few minutes later a porter arrived to take their luggage, then Jess and the nurse supported a very shaky Emily on the short distance to the lift.

"I feel like a new-born lamb," gasped Emily, wincing as the familiar pain gripped her ribs. She leaned gratefully against Jess as the lift descended.

"You'll soon be stronger," said Jess firmly, catching Anna's eye anxiously for confirmation.

The nurse nodded benignly. "A few days of fresh air and rest will see much improvement."

Lorenzo was waiting for them in the foyer, dressed more casually than usual, and to Jess's eyes so irresistible she wanted to throw herself into his arms there and then, regardless of the staff gathered to expedite their departure.

*"Buon giorno!"* he said, smiling at all three of them, but the quickly veiled look he gave Jess told her he was

controlling a similar impulse to her own. "How are you feeling this morning, Miss Emily?"

"Fine," she said manfully, but even with Jess holding her tightly by the arm it was obvious to everyone that this was a polite lie.

"Actually, Lorenzo," said Jess in an undertone, "she's not too good. Is it far to the car?"

"No. It waits outside." He turned to Anna and gave her some swift instructions, then, with a smile at Emily, said *"Permesso,"* and picked her up, telling Jess to follow them as he carried the invalid outside and down the red-carpeted steps to the car. He settled Emily gently in the back seat alongside Anna, held the front passenger door for Jess, then excused himself to go back into the hotel to talk to the manager.

"Are you all right, love?" Jess turned anxiously to peer at her friend.

"Of course I am." Emily smiled valiantly. "How could I be anything else with all this star treatment?"

Lorenzo Forli drove out of Florence with due care for the welfare of the invalid, and after a short journey on the autostrada turned off on to a quiet minor road, slowing down to allow his passengers time to admire the views. The narrow, winding route was lined in places with groups of flame-shaped cypresses used as windbreaks for the olive groves and vines grown on the slopes of rolling amber hills. Here and there a patch of brighter gold indicated a crop of sunflowers, and in some places Lorenzo pointed out fields of the barley and maize used to feed cattle and poultry.

Jess was entranced by it all, smiling radiantly in response to the occasional questioning glance Lorenzo sent in her direction. It amazed her that in such a short distance from the sophistication of Florence they were deep in a timeless landscape which seemed little changed from those in the Renaissance paintings she'd seen in the Uffizi.

A few kilometres later Lorenzo turned off on a much narrower road which he informed them was one of the *strade vicinali*, the neighbourhood roads which wander over the Italian countryside. This one was little more than a track which wound up to the summit of one of the rounded hills, where the car nosed through a gap in a ring of cypresses to bring them to a house very different from the formal, classical villa Jess had expected. Lorenzo's country home was a long, two-storey house with cinnamon roof tiles and white-shuttered windows, the natural stone of the walls gilded by the morning sun. There were outbuildings in the background, and big earthenware pots of geraniums stood in a paved courtyard where a table and several chairs sheltered under a group of trees from the heat of the Tuscan sun.

"How lovely!" exclaimed Emily.

"Villa Fortuna," announced Lorenzo. He looked at Jess, a question in his eyes. "You approve?"

"How could I not?" she said with fervour. "It's heavenly!"

Then there was a commotion as a small, plump woman came hurrying from the house, followed by a thin, dark man, both of them talking at once to welcome the lord of the manor and his guests.

Lorenzo jumped out of the car, smiling broadly in return, and suddenly Jess saw a different side of him. This was the man who'd been born here, and these the exuberant, affectionate couple who had known him from his birth. He greeted them with warm affection, then presented Jess to them with a proprietary air no one watching could fail to interpret.

"This is Carla, who cooks like an angel from heaven," he told her, "and Mario who takes care of everything else." He translated rapidly, bring much bridling laughter from the woman and a pleased smile from her husband.

Jess held out her hand. *"Piacere,"* she said, with as good an accent as she could muster.

Her essay into Italian brought forth an incomprehensible stream of it in return, though the gist of it was easy enough to understand. The fact that Signor Lorenzo had brought guests to stay was the cause of much happiness for Carla and Mario Monti, and much sympathy for a white-faced Emily when, despite her protests that she could walk, Lorenzo carried her from the car to one of the shaded chairs.

*"La poverina!"* said Carla with sympathy, then hurried off to fetch refreshments, taking Anna with her while her husband saw to the luggage.

"We shall sit here for a few minutes," said Lorenzo, pulling up a chair for Jess. "It is not too hot for you, Emily?"

"Not in the least," she assured him. "Besides, there's a lovely cool breeze here."

"We Tuscans build our houses on top of hills for just this purpose," he assured her, and turned to Jess. "And you, Jessamy? How do you feel?"

Knowing that Lorenzo meant a great deal more than whether she'd survived the journey without ill effect, Jess smiled at him luminously, and leaned back in her chair with a sigh of pleasure. "I feel wonderful," she assured him, and waved at the view. "I'd be happy just to sit here all day, gazing at this fabulous landscape. When I stayed with Leo I never went outside the city."

"I am pleased you like my home." He looked up with a smile for Carla, who was returning with a tray of coffee and almond biscuits recently taken from the oven. *"Grazie,"* he said as she put it down in front of Jess, then listened, nodding in approval, as Carla spoke at length before bestowing a smile on the guests and hurrying back into the house.

"Anna is putting your clothes away, Emily," he reported. "And the nurse says that once you have finished your coffee you must rest on your bed, so that you will feel strong enough to join us for lunch."

Jess grinned at the mutinous expression on her friend's face. "Anna's quite a tyrant, isn't she? But she's right, Em. Take it easy for a while."

"I will." Emily smiled ruefully. "In fact I'll be quite glad to lie down again. Feeble, isn't it?"

"You cannot expect to recover from *la pleurite* overnight," said Lorenzo gently. "Soon, once the medication has had more time to take effect, I shall take you exploring with Jessamy." He stood up. "But for the moment forgive me if I leave you for a while to speak with Mario."

When he'd gone Jess poured coffee with a steady hand, aware that Emily was watching her speculatively. "What?" she asked, adding cream and sugar.

"When you said all that about truly, madly, deeply and so on," began Emily in an undertone.

"Yes."

"Lorenzo feels the same about you, doesn't he?"

Jess smiled happily as she sat back with her coffee. "He says he does."

Emily pulled a face. "Which makes the situation a tad awkward for me, old love."

Jess shot a surprised glance at her. "Why?"

"Would *you* like playing gooseberry if the situation were reversed?"

Jess was quiet for a moment, trying to find words of reassurance. She took her sunglasses off and leaned forward to emphasise her words. "Actually, Em, it doesn't matter whether we're alone or not. To be in love with someone doesn't mean one has to *make* love."

"Not for you, Snow Queen, I know. But for most people it does."

Jess smiled crookedly. "Actually it does for me, too. This time."

Emily chuckled. "I thought as much. We've lived together for quite a while, Jess Dysart, but I've never seen you like this before."

"I know. But don't worry. I'm happy just as long as Lorenzo's somewhere near at hand. I promise there'll be no embarrassing displays of affection," Jess assured her. "Besides," she added, "there's not only you, but Anna, Carla and Mario, to name but a few. And Lorenzo said his sister, Isabella, will come rushing to inspect us when she discovers he's got guests."

"Is that a habit of hers?"

"Apparently he's never brought anyone to stay before. A woman, I mean."

Emily whistled softly, and held out her cup for more coffee. "Which means, I hazard a guess, that Signor Forli's intentions are strictly honourable where you're concerned."

Jess wasn't listening. She was smiling in a way which plainly dazzled the man who came to join them. "Is everything all right, Lorenzo?"

"Yes," he said simply, taking the chair beside her. "Everything." His eyes detached themselves from hers with an effort, which plainly delighted the third member of the trio. "How are you feeling, Emily?"

"She's feeling awkward," said Jess bluntly.

Emily went scarlet and Lorenzo frowned.

"Awkward?" he queried.

"She feels she's playing gooseberry," Jess informed him.

Lorenzo thought for a moment, mentally translating the unfamiliar term, then his face cleared, and he smiled at Emily with such warmth her colour receded a little. "Ah! I see." He nodded. "Jessamy has told you that she—she cares for me, no?"

"Yes," said Emily. "But she put it a lot more strongly than that."

Lorenzo exchanged a gleaming look with Jess, then turned back to her friend. "I shall be frank. I fell in love with Jessamy the moment I first saw her. And I consider myself the most fortunate of men, because last night she told me—"

"That it was the same for me," interrupted Jess. "And for the very first time, as you know better than anyone, Em."

"I do indeed. I'm very happy for you." Emily beamed on them both, then turned away a little to cough painfully. "Sorry. I think maybe it's time I found that bed. And not," she added breathlessly, "because I feel in the way. I just feel a bit weary."

Jess looked at her watch. "And in a few minutes it's time for the next dose of pills. Lorenzo, could you show us where we're to sleep?"

"Of course." He went over to Emily. "Come. I shall carry you upstairs."

"No, really!" she protested, looking horrified. "I can walk."

"Let us see how you are once you are inside," he compromised, and took her arm while Jess held on to the other.

Inside the house it was cool, and both Lorenzo's guests exclaimed with pleasure at the sight of gleaming tiled floors and stone walls, with arched doorways leading off the large hall into the various ground-floor rooms. A mixture of comfortable modern furniture lived in harmony with antique pieces, giving a very different effect from the formality of Lorenzo's apartment in the hotel.

"You shall explore the rooms later," he said, looking down into Emily's suddenly wan face as she eyed the flight of stone stairs which led to the upper floor. *"Permesso,"* he said again, and picked her up, leaving Jess to follow behind as he carried her friend to a room situated at the back of the house, with a view of the rolling countryside from its windows.

Anna was already there, setting out bottles of water and fruit juice on a table beside the wrought-iron bed, where crisp white covers were turned down in invitation. The nurse clucked in alarm at the sight of Emily's face, scolding gently as Lorenzo lowered the invalid into a wicker chair under the open window.

"Run away and play, children," said Emily, managing a grin. "I'm in good hands."

"Let me help you undress," said Jess, but Anna should her head.

"No, *signorina,* I shall take care of Emily. She needs to rest, then perhaps she can join you for lunch. We shall see."

On the gallery which ran the length of the upper floor, Lorenzo led Jess to a room at the far end of the house. It was similar in size and furnishing to Emily's, complete with a small bathroom, but with a slightly different view. And, to Jess's dismay, she found that her belongings had been unpacked and neatly put away.

"This is lovely, but Anna shouldn't have bothered with my things as well," said Jess, embarrassed.

"It was Carla who unpacked for you, not Anna," he informed her, and smiled as he took her in his arms. The door of the bedroom was open, so that anyone who passed could see in, and the kiss Lorenzo gave her was fleeting, but so possessive Jess was left in no doubt that their relationship had taken a new turn. "Do you mind that she suspects how things are with us, *amore*?"

"You told her?"

"Officially, no." He shrugged, smiling. "But I have brought no woman here since my marriage, so she takes my relationship with you for granted. Does this trouble you?"

"Not in the least," Jess assured him. "Soon, when we're more used to the idea ourselves, the whole world can know."

Lorenzo took her on a quick tour of the upper rooms, one of which was Roberto's when he cared to use it instead of his apartment in the city. Downstairs there was a big, formal room Lorenzo called a *salone*, beyond it a dining room and a *salotto*, an informal sitting room with comfortable, well-worn furniture. Finally Lorenzo showed Jess a room he used as a study, complete with the latest technology to keep him in touch with the family business when he was at the villa. Carla and Mario, he informed her, lived in the cottage outside at the back of the house, but during the day Carla reigned over their last port of call, the all-important kitchen. It was very large, filled with fragrant smells of the meal Carla was preparing with the help of a young girl Lorenzo introduced as Gina, Carla's niece.

Lorenzo conducted a rapid, teasing conversation with

Carla, then Jess said her goodbyes after miming her rapture at the enticing smells in the air.

"She loves you very much, Lorenzo," said Jess as they went outside into the courtyard.

"When I was young she was my nursemaid," he explained, "so for Carla I have always been her special charge."

"Did she go with you to Oltrarno when you married Renata?" asked Jess.

Lorenzo shook his head, looking bleak. "She wished to. But by this time Carla had been cook and housekeeper here for years, and my mother could not spare her, thank God. Otherwise I would have been forced to break Carla's heart by refusing to let her work for us. I could not have hidden the misery of my marriage from her."

Jess frowned. "But if she knows you that well she must have seen that your marriage was unhappy, darling."

The endearment won Jess a kiss before Lorenzo drew her down on a wicker sofa beside him.

"You are right, of course. Carla knew very well that my marriage was a failure. But not why. No one knows this, *carissima*. Only you."

To give Emily time to recover from the journey, lunch was served late in the cool dining room, by which time Jess was as ready as Lorenzo for the plates of steaming pasta put before them, rich with tomato and basil and scattered with pine nuts and crisp-fried morsels of pancetta.

Emily, who looked a lot better for her rest, ate more than Jess had expected, exclaiming over the heavenly flavour.

Lorenzo looked on with indulgent approval as Jess

wiped a hunk of crusty bread round her plate to enjoy the last scrap of sauce. "Do you know, Emily, that our dinner last night was the first meal I had seen Jessamy eat?" he remarked.

Emily stared at him in astonishment. "Really? But normally she—"

"Eats like a horse," said Jess, resigned, and grinned at Lorenzo. "I told you that, but you didn't believe me. And until last night we hadn't actually shared a proper meal, remember."

"You ate nothing of the meal served to us on the plane," he reminded her.

"She never does. She hates flying," Emily informed him.

Lorenzo eyed Jess in surprise. "You said nothing, *carissima*. You should have told me."

"I wasn't nervous this time."

"With Lorenzo for company you probably forgot you were even in a plane," said Emily, chuckling.

Jess made a face at her. "Something like that."

"I am flattered," said Lorenzo, looking unashamedly smug.

When Carla came in with dessert she smiled in satisfaction when Lorenzo translated his guests' appreciation.

"She says that's the way to get well, Emily," said Lorenzo, then exchanged a look with Jess when Carla placed a familiar cake in front of her before going back to the kitchen.

"That looks yummy," said Emily, then looked at the other two with narrowed eyes. "What's wrong?"

"Nothing," said Jess hastily. "Just a coincidence. We were given this for pudding last night."

"Is it nice?" asked Emily, as Jess served her with a modest slice.

"She did not eat it," said Lorenzo, poker-faced.

To avoid explanations Jess cut a piece for herself, but Lorenzo refused.

"It is not cake that I want," he informed her, smiling into her eyes. "Just a little of this cheese to eat with Carla's bread," he added innocently.

Emily, plainly aware of undercurrents, tactfully ignored her friend's hot cheeks and applied herself to the cake. "It's gorgeous," she pronounced. "What's in it?"

"Almonds, lemon and ricotta," said Jess promptly, tasting her own. "And you're right. It's delicious."

After dinner that first evening Emily asked permission to ring her mother. "In case she rings the hotel and finds I've vanished! But I didn't want to ring until I at least sounded better."

"Invite your mother to come and stay here with you until you are well," suggested Lorenzo. "After helping with the little ones she must also be in need of rest."

Emily, though deeply grateful for Lorenzo Forli's kindness, flatly refused to take advantage of it to such an extent. "In fact," she added, "I should be fit enough to return with Jess on Saturday."

"Are you sure you're up to that on your own?" said Jess.

"*This* Saturday?" said Lorenzo swiftly, eyes narrowed. "You did not tell me, Jessamy."

Jess looked at him in distress. "I just have to get back next week because other people at the agency are on holiday. Could you arrange a flight for me?"

After Emily had gone off to ring her mother Lorenzo seized Jess by the shoulders. "Stay with me. Tell this agency of yours that you are not returning."

"I must go back, darling. Please—don't look at me

like that; I can't bear it." To her dismay Jess began to sob, and Lorenzo swept her into his arms.

"I cannot endure your tears," he said huskily. "So. I shall let you go back. But not for long. If you love me—"

"I do, I do," she assured him passionately.

"Then resign at once. And I shall come to England and ask your father's permission to marry his daughter," Lorenzo said with decision, and kissed her hard by way of emphasis.

By the time Emily rejoined them they were drinking coffee in the small sitting room, Jess composed and harmony restored.

"The little girls are better," Emily reported, and sat down rather wearily.

"How did your mother take the news about the pleurisy?" asked Jess, passing her a cup of coffee.

"Not terribly well. On top of the chicken pox it was a bit much, poor dear."

"She is naturally anxious," said Lorenzo. "It is Anna's opinion that you will not be well enough to travel on Saturday, Emily. Ask your mother to join you here in a day or two. Next week, after Jessamy has gone, I shall return to the apartment in Firenze. You may have the house to yourselves, except for Carla and Mario, of course."

But Emily wouldn't hear of it. "It's very kind of you, Lorenzo, but I must go back with Jess," she said firmly. "I already feel much better—"

"Well, you don't look it," said Jess flatly, but just then Anna appeared and put an end to the discussion by stating that it was time her patient was in bed.

Later Jess went out into the courtyard with Lorenzo, to look at the stars in the cool of the evening. "I wish I could stay," she said wistfully.

"Soon you shall stay with me for ever!"

"Will we live here all the time?" asked Jess.

"Some of the time only." Lorenzo put his arm round her and drew her close. "We shall spend our weekends here, the rest of the time at the *appartamento*." He rubbed his cheek against her hair. "There are occasions when I curse living so close to my work, but last night I gave thanks for such an arrangement," he whispered, his breath warm against her skin.

"So did I," she whispered back, and turned her face up for his kiss.

To her surprise Jess soon found she was as tired as Emily. "I don't know why," she said apologetically, after a second yawn. "Heaven knows I haven't done much today."

"It is the air," said Lorenzo, pulling her to her feet.

"And I had a very strenuous day yesterday—" Jess halted, biting her lip, and Lorenzo laughed softly and held her close.

"We should have such strenuous days more often, *tesoro*."

Jess was pensive as they went in the house. "The thing is, Lorenzo," she said, as he began turning out lights, "Emily won't ask her mother to come because Mrs Shaw is a widow on a pension. She just wouldn't have the spare cash for the flight."

"Ah, I see!" Lorenzo frowned. "It would be simple to buy a ticket. But how can we arrange it so that the lady is not offended?"

"Tomorrow I'll ring Celia, Emily's sister, and see what can be done."

When Emily was resting after lunch next day Jess made her phone call and found that Celia thought a trip to Tuscany was an excellent idea for her mother. After a

rapid consultation with her husband Celia reported that
Daddy was taking a fortnight off to help with the con-
valescence, and would be very happy to provide an air-
line ticket to Pisa for Mrs Shaw as a gift for all her hard
work.

"Or maybe Jack wants his mother-in-law out of the
way now he's home," said Emily privately to Jess, after
her mother rang in great excitement to say that she would
soon be on her way to Italy.

"Don't they get on?" asked Jess.

"Reasonably well. But Jack works long hours, so he
doesn't see much of his family during the week. He'll be
glad of time alone with them. Nothing more sinister than
that. I hope." Emily sipped her iced fruit juice, frowning.
"It seems so hard on you, though, Jess. You're back to
the grind, while I'm staying on here where you should
be. How are you going to tear yourself away from
Lorenzo?"

"With the utmost difficulty," said Jess despondently.

"Tell me to mind my own business, but has he popped
the question yet?"

"Yes. But that's not for publication yet, Em. To anyone."

Emily's grey eyes opened wide. "You said yes, of
course—" She breathed in sharply, and began to cough,
and Anna came hurrying to suggest her patient went in-
doors where it was cooler.

"You stay here, Jess," said Emily when she could
speak. "I think I'll go and have a bath, then read for a
while on my bed."

"Not suffering from gooseberry complex by any
chance?" demanded Jess suspiciously.

Emily grinned and went off with Anna, leaving Jess
alone to gaze at the view. It would be agony to part with

Lorenzo, she knew very well, there was no possible way out of it. And she would need to warn her family about his proposal before he contacted them himself. Jess tried to imagine the general Dysart reaction to the news, and decided to ask Lorenzo to leave it for a while before breaking it to them, so that the whole idea didn't smack of unseemly haste.

"You are very thoughtful," said Lorenzo, coming to sit beside her. He took her hand and kissed it. "You look sad, *piccola*."

"I feel sad," she admitted. "I don't want to go back on Saturday, Lorenzo."

"When do you start work?"

"Monday," she said gloomily.

"Then stay until Sunday. Once Emily's mother arrives you have no need to stay here at the villa." Lorenzo's eyes lit with the look which never failed to send heat rushing through her every vein. "We could leave here on Saturday morning, then stay in Firenze until it is time for you to leave."

Jess buried her face against his shoulder. "Yes, please," she said in a muffled voice. "I'd like that *very* much."

*"Bene!"* he said with satisfaction. "Because I have already asked my assistant to make the reservation for Sunday."

"You were so very sure I'd want to stay?"

Lorenzo gave his very Latin shrug. "Why should you be in London alone, I in Firenze alone, when we can be together for an extra day? Guido will fax me shortly with confirmation of your flight."

Jess looked after him with a wry little smile as Lorenzo strode into the house to wait for the fax. Lorenzo Forli was used to getting his own way. Though in this instance

it was very much her own way, too. He was right. She
wouldn't have time to get down to Friars Wood and back.
And to spend Saturday night and Sunday on her own in
London was madness when the alternative was extra time
with Lorenzo. Alone with Lorenzo, she reminded herself,
and gave an ecstatic little shiver at the thought of it.

Jess had fully expected her stay at the Villa Fortuna to
be frustrating, since there would be little opportunity to
be alone with Lorenzo, and even when they were the
likelihood of interruption would prevent anything other
than hand-holding and a kiss or two. But in some strange
way she soon found she liked the arrangement very
much. After rushing headlong into the ultimate intimacy
with Lorenzo Forli it was strangely satisfying to back-
track a little, just to be together, whether alone or not. It
was a joy just to walk with him, to explore the property,
or to sit and talk under the trees in the courtyard. He
began teaching her a little basic Italian, but otherwise
their time alone together was spent in a voyage of discovery.

"To make up for all the years before you came into
my life," declared Lorenzo.

And at night, when Lorenzo escorted her upstairs to
her room, long after Emily had retired to hers, he kissed
Jess at length before they parted, but after the first day
had never set foot in her room. Knowing he was in the
bedroom next to hers, Jess had expected to spend restless,
sleepless nights. Instead she slept soundly and woke
early, eager to join Lorenzo for the breakfast Carla served
them in the courtyard before the sun grew too fierce.
Emily breakfasted in bed, happy to give Jess time alone
with Lorenzo.

Late in the afternoon Jess was reading alone in the

courtyard while Emily had a rest, and Lorenzo was in his study dealing with hotel business over the phone. Jess looked up from her book at the sound of an approaching car, the sound growing louder in the stillness, indicating that the driver was heading for the Villa Fortuna, since the narrow track led only to the house.

When a car appeared through the cypresses Jess hesitated, wondering whether to go and find Lorenzo, or stand her ground and greet the visitor herself. In which case, she thought wryly, it was to be hoped that the visitor spoke English. The few words of Italian she'd learned so far were better suited to the bedroom than to welcoming guests.

A slim, bespectacled young man got out of the car, then reached inside it for a medical bag. Dr Tosti had obviously come to check on the patient.

"How do you do?" said Jess with a smile, holding out her hand. "I'm Jessamy Dysart."

"*Piacere*, Miss Dysart," he said, bowing over her hand. "Bruno Tosti. Anna has reported to me that your friend is improving, but Lorenzo wishes me to confirm this."

Lorenzo came hurrying from the house, his smile wide as he wrung his friend's hand. "*Come sta*, Bruno? But we are obliged to converse in English. Jessamy has very little Italian yet."

Bruno Tosti was a very pleasant man, and obviously much attached to Lorenzo. He admitted that it had been no hardship to leave the city to come to Villa Fortuna, and since he was not on duty that evening he would be very glad to accept Lorenzo's invitation to dinner.

"I'll go and call Anna," volunteered Jess. "Emily is reading on her bed, but I expect you'd like to talk to the nurse first."

"Thank you, Jessamy," said Lorenzo. "Will you ask Carla to bring coffee?"

Jess hurried off to embark on a funny little exchange with Carla, half-mime, have words, and a great deal of hand-waving. Afterwards she ran up the smooth stone stairs to Emily's room, and found Anna changing the sheets while her patient sat curled up in a chair with her book.

"Anna, Dottore Tosti's here," said Jess breathlessly. "He'd like to see you before he examines the patient."

The nurse hurried off at once, and Emily sprang rashly to her feet.

"At least I'm clean," she said, equally breathless as she brushed her hair. "Last time the doctor saw me I was covered in sweat and thoroughly unappetising. And he's rather nice in a quiet sort of way, isn't he?"

"Just as well you approve," said Jess, grinning. "He's staying to dinner."

This information threw the patient into some confusion. "Not that it matters what I wear," she groaned. "I'm not exactly at my best at the moment."

"Maybe the doctor won't let you stay up for dinner," teased Jess.

However, after a thorough examination of the patient, during which both the nurse and Jess were present, the doctor pronounced himself pleased with Emily's progress, but ordered a great deal of rest, and approved her decision to stay on at the villa for an extra week.

"This is good," he informed her. "It would be most unwise to fly home on Saturday, as Lorenzo told me you intended, *signorina*. But with your mother to look after you once Anna has gone, after another week of rest you should be fully recovered."

It was a quietly festive little party which gathered in

the courtyard before dinner. Emily and the rather serious young doctor got on very well, and Jess was left free to enjoy her proximity to Lorenzo, and contribute to the conversation now and then, but was mostly content just to sit near him, sipping her glass of wine sparingly, and savouring this new-found bliss she could hardly believe was hers.

When another car was heard approaching up the steep, winding bends to the villa, Lorenzo smiled with sudden pleasure as an Alfa Romeo Spider materialised through the cypresses, and came to a dramatic halt. A familiar figure jumped out and came striding towards them, a broad grin on his handsome face.

*"Buona sera!* I am in time for dinner?''

# CHAPTER TEN

ROBERTO FORLI kissed Jess on both cheeks, hugged his brother, shook hands with the doctor, then turned the full wattage of his smile on Emily and demanded an introduction.

Jess felt sudden sympathy for the sober doctor. His animation diminished visibly as he witnessed his patient's reaction to the confident charm of Roberto Forli. Carla came bustling out of the house, stopped short dramatically, hand on heart, as she laid eyes on Roberto, and let forth a stream of scolding he responded to by taking her in his arms and hugging her until she relented at last and smiled lovingly on him.

Roberto excused himself to tidy up and went off with Carla, an arm slung round her shoulders as he offered extravagant apologies she responded to by patting his cheek as they went into the house.

"Did you know Roberto was back?" asked Jess.

"No." Lorenzo shrugged negligently. "But it is always so. He arrives unannounced. Carla gives him a furious lecture. Then she serves him food fit for a king."

"Does she ever scold you, Lorenzo?" asked Emily mischievously.

"Never," he said piously, eyes dancing. "I am much too virtuous!"

"Modest, too," said Jess, laughing, then turned to Bruno Tosti and drew him into the conversation.

When Roberto returned he helped Emily to her feet and escorted her into dinner, leaving the doctor to follow behind with Jess and Lorenzo. Roberto, thought Jess, amused, had obviously recovered his spirits since last seen leaving her sister's wedding in deep dejection.

While they enjoyed Carla's wild mushroom risotto Roberto Forli informed them he had just arrived from London that day.

"To find a message waiting for me from Isabella," he went on, with a significant look at his brother. "She arrived home today from her little holiday with her friend in Positano in much excitement, Lorenzo, because you told Andrea that Jess and her friend stay at the villa. So I decided to join you for dinner."

"Isabella did not insist on coming with you?" said Lorenzo dryly, pouring wine.

Roberto laughed. "After living without her for a week Andrea desires his wife's presence tonight. But tomorrow she will no doubt arrive before breakfast!" He explained to Emily that Isabella took a very keen interest in the lives of her brothers, her greatest ambition in life to see them both happily married.

"My sister's just the same with me," she said, smiling.

"You have no wish for this, Emily?" asked Bruno.

"Oh, yes," she said airily. "One day. But not yet."

He eyed the portion of risotto left on her plate. "You must eat, or you will not get well."

"If I eat any more I won't manage the next course," said Emily apologetically, and asked Lorenzo to explain to Carla. "She's so kind. I wouldn't hurt her for the world."

"You may eat as much, or as little, as you like," he assured her.

"Drink some wine instead," urged Roberto.

"No, she must not," said Bruno quickly. "Mineral water only, Roberto, because of her medication."

The evening had been convivial before Roberto's arrival, but his presence was a catalyst which changed the occasion into a party. He kept them entertained with tales of his stay in London while they ate thin slivers of pork grilled with lemon, rosemary and garlic, followed by a confection of chestnut purée and whipped cream. But at last Emily, though very obviously enjoying herself enormously, began to look tired. At which point Bruno Tosti took unconcealed satisfaction in scoring points off Roberto, even if it meant depriving himself of his patient's company.

"And now, Miss Emily," he said formally, once coffee had been served, "it is time you retired to your bed."

"At this hour?" protested Roberto, then caught the look Lorenzo gave him, and threw up his hands in surrender. "Emily is your patient, of course, Bruno."

*"Esattamente,"* agreed the doctor stiffly. "And to recover sufficiently to fly home next week it is essential she takes much rest."

Emily got up at once. "You're right, doctor," she said, smiling as she held out her hand to him. "Thank you so much for coming to see me." She turned to Roberto. "It was very nice to meet you, too."

*"Prego!"* He kissed her hand, then straightened, smiling. "But you will do so again in the morning, Emily. I am staying the night."

After Emily's round of goodnights the two women went out together, leaving, Jess suspected, rather an awkward silence behind them.

"How are you feeling, really?" she asked, as she took Emily's arm to mount the stairs. "Are you up for this, or shall I call for some muscles from your rivals down there? Which do you fancy? Roberto's the hunkier of the two."

Emily laughed breathlessly, then regretted it as the familiar pain caught her. "I can make my own way tonight, thanks," she gasped at last. "If we—keep—to a crawl!"

Before they'd negotiated more than a couple of steps Anna came hurrying down towards them to take Emily's other arm.

"It is late," she scolded, "and you should be in bed, *cara*. I could not interrupt when Dottore Tosti was there, but I was most worried."

"Sorry, Anna." Emily smiled at the nurse apologetically. "I should have come earlier, but I was having such a good time." She turned to Jess. "Off you go, back to the fray."

Jess gave her a hug and a kiss, wished her a restful night, then went back downstairs to find Lorenzo and Roberto alone in the courtyard. They both got to their feet as she joined them, and Lorenzo informed her that Bruno sent his apologies, but had been obliged to leave.

"I think I spoil the evening for Bruno," said Roberto, without any noticeable penitence. "Let us be comfortable in the *salotto*. Will you have some grappa, Jess?"

"No, thanks." Jess sat down on a small sofa beside Lorenzo, who took her hand in his and held it there.

"Roberto," he said, lifting Jess's hand to his lips. "I have asked Jessamy to marry me."

Roberto looked stunned for a moment, then his eyes lit up with pure delight, and he got up to kiss Jess on both cheeks. "*Ottimo!* From the look of triumph on my brother's face, *cara*, I assume you have consented?"

She nodded. "You probably think this is all very sudden. Do you approve?" she added bluntly.

Roberto gave his brother a drink, then sat down opposite with his own, grinning as he raised his hand in blessing. "If Lorenzo is happy of course I approve. I think my brother is a fortunate man.'' He shrugged. ''But it is no real surprise, Jess. After years of trying to interest him in various charming ladies, with no success at all, one day he saw your photograph and—'' He snapped his fingers. ''That was that.''

The telephone rang in the hall and Lorenzo got up, excusing himself as he went to answer it. When they were alone, Robert leaned forward, his eyes bright with urgency.

''My brother was greatly affected by his wife's death, Jess,'' he said rapidly in an undertone. ''He may not have told you this. He has never discussed it. But for a long time afterwards he was like a man turned to stone. It has taken him a very long time to recover, and I would not see him hurt again, you understand. You are sure of your feelings for him, Jess? In such a short time?''

''Utterly certain.'' Jess gave him a very straight look. ''I never imagined something so wonderful would ever happen to me.''

Eyes softened, Roberto sat back in undisguised relief. ''*Bene!* Then I welcome you to our family with a glad heart.'' He paused, staring down into his drink. ''Does your—your family know?''

Knowing he really meant Leonie, Jess shook her head. ''No. I need time to get used to the idea myself first.''

''Naturally.'' Roberto looked up with a smile as his brother returned. ''Isabella?''

''No, the hotel. A small crisis which demands my presence for a while tomorrow.'' Lorenzo shrugged ruefully, and resumed his place by Jess. ''I must leave you for a few hours in the morning, *carissima*. But I shall return to you as soon as I can.''

* * *

After the excitement of the dinner party Emily was glad to stay in bed next morning, and sent her goodbyes via Jess, who breakfasted with the brothers before they drove off separately to Florence.

"You must also rest, *carissima*," said Lorenzo, once Roberto had gone. "I shall be home this afternoon, I promise."

"I'll miss you," she said huskily, as she walked with him to the car, and Lorenzo took her in his arms and held her tightly.

"I am very glad that you will miss me!" he said against her lips and kissed her, leaving Jess to wave forlornly as he drove off.

Anna came hurrying out into the courtyard to inform Jess that the invalid had gone back to sleep after her breakfast. "The evening exhausted her. She is not as strong yet as she believes," said the nurse darkly. "Dottore Tosti has asked me to stay until Emily's mother arrives to look after her."

Jess thanked her, then sat under the trees with a book, smiling to herself. Bruno Tosti obviously thought she couldn't be trusted to look after her friend herself, even though she'd done it before often enough, due to Emily's habit of catching any bug going the rounds during winter.

In some ways Jess felt glad to be alone for a while, just to sit and think over the past few days. Love at first sight was possible, she knew very well from Leo and Jonah, but she had never, in her wildest dreams, expected to experience it herself. On the rare occasions when marriage had actually figured in her thoughts, she'd visualised some steady, affectionate man who would make a good husband and father. But all that had changed the day she first set eyes on Lorenzo Forli. She stretched out on the couch she normally shared with him, so lost in daydreams she was startled when Carla touched her shoulder gently and mimed a telephone call.

"Lorenzo?" said Jess hopefully, jumping up.

Carla shook her head, smiling indulgently, and said very clearly, "Signora Moretti—Isabella!"

Jess went in the house and picked up the telephone from a marble table in the hall, clearing her throat a little nervously before she said a cautious hello.

"This is Isabella Moretti, sister of Lorenzo. You are Jessamy?" said an attractive voice more heavily accented than either of her brothers'.

"Yes, I am. How do you do?"

"*Piacere!* Carla says he has gone to Firenze, and you are alone. I hope I did not disturb you."

"No, indeed. How nice of you to ring. Roberto said you might come to the villa today."

"This is why I call, *cara*. I would so much like to meet you, but I know your friend has been ill. Would it disturb her if I come to lunch?"

"Not at all," said Jess with complete truth. Emily would be agog. "We'd both be delighted. Are you bringing your little boys?"

Isabella laughed, a husky, joyous sound very like Roberto's. "No, no. That would be much too much for everyone. They are in school. You shall meet them another time. Tell Carla I arrive at noon. *Ciao!*"

Jess went into the kitchen to inform Carla, with a great deal of hand-waving, that Isabella was coming to lunch, then went upstairs to find the invalid up and dressed.

Emily turned from the mirror to smile at her, hairbrush in hand. "Feeling blue without Lorenzo?

"I was." Jess admitted, grinning. "But we'll soon have diversion, ducky. Signora Isabella Moretti is coming to lunch!"

Emily laughed. "Not breakfast, then?"

"No. And at least she warned us first. I'm off for a shower." Jess eyed herself in the mirror without pleasure. "Just look at my hair—I was mad to have it cut so short."

"Very stylish, dearie, as you well know, so go and do magic with a hot brush, and I'll creep downstairs to the courtyard to read." Emily grinned. "Don't worry, Anna's given permission!"

Jess eyed her friend's face closely. "You certainly look better than you did last night, Em. Too much excitement, obviously, especially when Roberto turned up."

"Probably—he's very different from big brother!"

"Of course," retorted Jess. "Lorenzo's unique."

Certain that Isabella Moretti would be the picture of Italian chic, Jess worked on her hair until it gleamed, and dressed in black linen trousers and a cream silk shirt, with a plaited black leather belt Leonie had once brought her from the shops near the Santa Croce in Florence.

"Very classy," said Emily, when Jess joined her in the courtyard. "None of the babes you hire for the agency could do better."

"Thank you for those kind words." Jess pulled a face. "Silly, I know, but I'm nervous."

"How old is this famous Isabella?"

"She's the youngest, so late twenties, I suppose." Jess looked round with a smile as young Gina came out, carrying a tray with a pitcher and glasses. "*Grazie*, Gina."

"I pleaded with Anna for a change from mineral water," said Emily, inspecting the ice-filled jug. "This, by the look of it, is fresh lemonade—bliss!"

When a car was heard soon afterwards Jess put down her glass and got to her feet, inwardly bracing herself as a sleek white roadster appeared through the cypresses. "You stay there, invalid. I'll do the necessary."

The driver slid from the car the moment it stopped, whipping off scarf and sunglasses to smile as she hurried forward, her dark eyes bright with animation.

"You are Jessamy," said the new arrival, and seized Jess by the shoulders and kissed her on both cheeks.

Isabella Moretti was a feminine, curvy version of her brother Roberto, her hair cut to hang in a skilful bell-shape about her face.

"How nice to meet you," said Jess, responding involuntarily to the visitor's unaffected warmth. Isabella Moretti was just as elegant as imagined, in a starkly plain beige linen dress, her matching shoes a miracle of Florentine craft, her jewellery limited to a pair of rings and a watch set in a gold bracelet which hung loose from her wrist. "Please come and meet my friend, Emily Shaw."

Emily got up to extend her hand in greeting, and said a rather shy hello.

"*Piacere!* Sit, please," said Isabella, and took the hand, but also kissed both of Emily's still-wan cheeks. "Such bad luck to be ill on holiday."

"I've been very fortunate to come here to get better, *signora.*"

"Isabella, *per favore!*"

"Will you have some lemonade?" said Jess, wondering if she should offer coffee instead, but reluctant to sound too territorial in the house that had once been Isabella's home. And still was, in some ways.

Isabella was very happy to drink lemonade. She tossed her fabulously beautiful handbag on the table and took a chair next to Jess, leaving the sofa to Emily. "Lie there and rest, *cara,*" she advised. "You look pale."

"We had rather a lively evening," Jess informed her,

and smiled at Emily. "Dr Tosti came to visit the invalid, then stayed on to dinner—"

"And Roberto joined you, of course." Isabella laughed. "He told me he would. But you, of course, Jessamy—" She paused. "Does everyone call you that?"

"No," said Emily. "Only Lorenzo. To the rest of the world she's known as Jess."

Isabella plainly found this bit of information fascination. "Then I shall call you this, also, and leave your special name to my brother. But, Jess, you know Roberto already, of course. Before you met Lorenzo."

"My sister and I had dinner with him when he came to England earlier in the year," agreed Jess.

Isabella cast her eyes skywards. "I know this! He was unbearable when he came home." She leaned nearer confidentially. "I was amazed when Roberto decided to attend her wedding. And now I find Lorenzo was there also. Is your sister happy, Jess?"

"Very. She's on her honeymoon, probably in the South of France by now."

"You approve of her husband?"

"Very much indeed." Jess smiled. "I've always been fond of Jonah."

"*Bene*! Tell Leonie I wish her well," said Isabella, and turned to Emily. "And you, *cara*, do you have a special man?"

Emily looked startled. "Er—no. No, I don't. Not at the moment."

Carla came hurrying out before there were more questions. Isabella jumped to her feet to embrace her, and embarked on a long, affectionate exchange before turning to the others in apology.

"Forgive me, but Carla always desires information

about my sons. Also she says lunch is ready inside. *Andiamo*."

Over a lunch of salad and *frittata*, Carla's perfect asparagus omelette, Isabella was only too happy to talk about Antonio and Claudio.

"They are enchanting, also, exhausting," she said, chuckling, "but I have a very good girl who helps with them, and now they are in school life is easier." She looked at her watch. "I must return in time for them to come home today, because I was away all last week with my friend Angelica, listening to her woes. She is a lawyer, and very clever, but unlucky in love!" Isabella rolled her eyes. "I was very happy to return to Andrea. He also is a lawyer, but when it comes to love—" She smiled engagingly. "He says he is a fortunate man."

Jess could well believe it. Isabella Moretti was a young woman of great charm and vivacity, and after an entire week without her Andrea Moretti had no doubt welcomed his wife home with open arms.

The three of them spent a very pleasant time together over lunch, but when it was over Emily got to her feet.

"Please excuse me, Isabella. I'd better go up for a rest, or Anna will scold. I'm so glad to have met you."

Isabella professed herself equally pleased, invited Emily to visit her in Lucca whenever she wished, then went out to the courtyard with Jess to drink coffee under the trees.

"How long do you stay, Jess?" she said, as she filled their cups, automatically taking on the role of hostess.

"Until Sunday, if Lorenzo can arrange it. I should be flying back on Saturday, but I don't start work until Monday, so—"

"So Lorenzo persuaded you to spend every minute

you could with him before leaving him,'' said Isabella, nodding. "What is this work, *cara*?''

Jess described her job at the agency, finding it very easy to talk to someone so fascinated by insight into the life of the successful model.

At last, with much regret, Isabella announced it was time for her to drive home. "But before I go," she added, her vivid face suddenly sober, "there is something I must say to you.''

Jess braced herself. "Yes?''

Isabella fiddled with her watch. "You know that Lorenzo has not had a—a real relationship with any woman since his wife died?''

"Yes. He told me.'' Jess smiled a little. "Roberto told me, too.''

Isabella made a face. "And now I am repeating it.'' She threw out her hands in appeal. "I have no wish to intrude on private feelings, *cara*, but after the tragedy of Renata I so want Lorenzo to be happy. I love him very much, you understand.''

"So do I,'' Jess assured her. "And to set your mind at rest, Isabella, I never, ever intend to cause him any hurt. In fact,'' she added, smiling radiantly, "Lorenzo has asked me to marry him and I've said yes.''

Isabella gave a squeal of excitement and jumped up to kiss Jess with wild enthusiasm. "*Meravigliso!* I am so glad. I must hurry home right away to call Andrea. Lorenzo must bring you to dine with us tomorrow. I shall ring him tonight. *Dio*, I am so happy for him. And for you, *cara*!'' She rushed into the house to say goodbye to Carla, then ran back out again to embrace Jess once again, gave good wishes for Emily's recovery, and drove away, waving until she was out of sight.

Jess sat alone for a long time afterwards, her eyes on

the rolling vine-clad hills. Isabella's reaction to her announcement had been gratifying in the extreme, Roberto's, too. But now it was time to ask for Dysart approval, which was something new for her parents. Jess had never taken any man home to Friars Wood, something they had found rather strange, she knew only too well. But they had taken very quickly to Lorenzo, which was a good start. Though perhaps they'd feel sad at losing another daughter to Italy, when the first had just returned home for good from Florence. But Jess was confident they would give her their blessing.

"You look very serious," teased a familiar voice, and Jess sprang to her feet and into Lorenzo's arms.

"You're early!" she exclaimed.

"Of course I am early," said Lorenzo at last, smiling down into her eyes. "This is a very special day."

"Every day since I've known you has been special." Jess rubbed her cheek against his. "What's different about today?"

Lorenzo held her away from him, frowning in mock indignation. "You have forgotten? This is our anniversary, *innamorata*, a whole week since I first saw you in the flesh!"

# CHAPTER ELEVEN

"AH, SUCH beautiful flesh," he murmured in her ear, and kissed her again, then frowned when he discovered she was crying. "Tears, Jessamy. Why?"

"Because you're so wonderful and I'm so happy," she said thickly, and smiled at him through the tears clinging to her lashes. "I can hardly believe it's only a week since I first saw you. Everything in life before then seems unimportant."

Lorenzo drew her down to the couch and put his arm round her. "Those are very rewarding words for a man to hear, *carissima*."

"But the truth," she assured him, sniffing inelegantly.

He reached in his pocket. "I have a present for you to mark the occasion."

Jess gazed in awe at the ring he produced. It was modern, a heavy gold band with a plain shank widening into a raised mound encrusted with small diamonds. Lorenzo slid it on her ring finger, and kissed it.

"This is just a token, not an *anello di fidanzato*, because we are not yet officially engaged. You can wear it on the other hand, if you wish. When I have your father's approval I shall buy you another, which we shall choose together. Do you like it? *Dio*, you are crying again!"

Jess flung her arms round his neck and kissed him, careless of the tears streaming down her face. "Darling, I love it. And I love you. I've missed you so much today. Lorenzo, I wish you could fly back with me."

"I, too," he said, kissing away her tears. "But this is

not possible for a week or so. I shall join you the moment I can, I swear.'' He looked up to smile at Emily, who was hovering in the doorway.

"Come. Join us," he said at once, getting to his feet.

"I don't want to intrude," she said awkwardly, "but I heard Jess crying. Is anything wrong?"

Jess smiled, sniffing hard, blissfully ignorant of mascara streaks under her eyes. "Come and sit down. Look!" She held out her hand. "Lorenzo just gave me this."

"And you're crying?" Emily shook her head. "I'd be over the moon if someone gave *me* a ring like that!"

"I did not bring you a ring, Emily," said Lorenzo, handing over a package. "But I think you may like this."

She gazed at him, horrified. "After all you've done for me I don't need presents!" Recalling her manners hurriedly, she thanked him and undid the parcel, her embarrassment changing to laughter when she held up a packet of Earl Grey tea. "Wonderful! Just what I need," she assured him.

Lorenzo went off to hand the tea over to Carla, and to change his formal suit for something more comfortable, and the three of them spent a relaxed afternoon together, Jess telling him how much they'd enjoyed meeting the vivacious Isabella.

"She's going to ring you tonight to invite us to dinner tomorrow," said Jess, "but it seems a shame to desert Mrs Shaw on her first evening here, especially when I'm leaving next day. Lorenzo, could you invite Isabella and her husband to dine here instead? Roberto, too, of course."

"You mustn't change your plans on my account," said Emily swiftly. "Mother would hate it if she thought she was causing any trouble."

Lorenzo smiled at her in reassurance. "Jessamy is right. I shall ring Isabella myself to suggest a change of plan, and tell her I am to do as she wishes and get married again."

"I've already told her," said Jess quickly. "I hope you don't mind, Lorenzo."

"Mind? I am delighted!"

"I just hope another dinner party won't be too much work for Carla."

Lorenzo laughed indulgently. "When I tell her we celebrate not only the arrival of Emily's mother but our own betrothal, *carissima*, Carla will be very, very happy to make a special dinner."

He was right. After a conversation with his sister after dinner Lorenzo went off to talk with Carla in the kitchen. She came hurrying back with him to kiss Jess and embrace her with exuberance, tears in her eyes as she professed her joy in a spate of words which needed no translation before she rushed off to give her husband the official news.

Emily went to bed soon afterwards, insisting she was tired out by all the excitement. Blessing her friend's tact, Jess spent the rest of the evening in the small sitting room with Lorenzo, her head on his shoulder as they made plans.

"I hope your family will receive the news with equal joy," said Lorenzo huskily, his cheek on her hair.

"I'm sure they will." Jess turned her head to meet his eyes. "But even in the unlikely event that they don't, nothing will change my mind, Lorenzo."

"*Carissima!*" He kissed her at length to show his appreciation. "I am delighted to hear this, of course, but I would prefer to receive your parents' blessing. I like them

both very much. And little Fenella, at least, will be most
pleased. She wishes to visit me here, remember."

Jess chuckled. "The moment she hears the news she'll
want to be bridesmaid again, too—" She frowned. "But
perhaps you'd rather not have a church ceremony this
time."

"Because of my first wedding?" Lorenzo shook his
head. "This time it will be very different for me. I would
like to marry in your charming little church, Jessamy.
Your parents would prefer this, no?"

"Of course they would." She looked at him questioningly. "What sort of date did you have in mind?"

"My choice would be tomorrow if we could!" He
kissed her hungrily and at once the urge to talk vanished,
replaced by desire so swift and overwhelming Jess surrendered herself to his mouth and hands with a lack of
inhibition which, in more private surroundings, would
have swiftly brought them to the inevitable conclusion.

"This is torture," Lorenzo said hoarsely. "If you love
me, Jessamy, for the love of God marry me soon. I need
you."

Shaken to the core by his plea, Jess held his head
against her breast, smoothing the dishevelled dark hair
until they were calmer. "Lorenzo," she whispered at last,
and he raised his head to look at her.

"Yes, *tesoro*?"

"On Saturday, shall we stay at your apartment in the
hotel?"

He sat up, his eyes narrowed to a triumphant gleam.
"No. We shall not."

Jess raised an eyebrow. "Where, then?"

"Isabella has offered us her house in Lucca for the
night. Andrea is taking his wife and sons to visit his
parents in Siena. They will return on Sunday morning,

just before we leave for the airport.'' He raised an eyebrow. ''You approve?''

Jess felt a tide of hot colour flood her face. ''You know I do,'' she muttered, and buried the offending face against his shoulder.

Lorenzo heaved in a deep, unsteady breath. ''Isabella takes pride in the room she keeps for visitors. I have slept there before. But always alone. This time—''

''This time you can hold me in your arms all night,'' said Jess in a muffled voice.

''My problem, *amore*, will be to let you go in the morning!''

Because Emily was still in no fit state to make the journey, next day Jess went with Lorenzo to fetch Mrs Shaw from the airport at Pisa, and sat in the back of the car with her to reassure her that Emily was improving fast. Janet Shaw looked tired and pale, but after expressing repeated thanks to Lorenzo grew very animated at the thought of her unexpected holiday to Italy, and exclaimed in delight at everything she saw on the journey. When they reached the Villa Fortuna Emily was sitting under the trees, waiting. Janet flew out of the car and rushed to embrace her daughter, and, leaving them to their tearful reunion, Lorenzo and Jess went inside the house to ask Carla to bring tea to refresh the weary traveller.

The evening was even livelier than the one before. To do justice to the occasion Jess wore a clinging black dress bought for her brother's twenty-first birthday party, with no jewellery other than the new ring, which she slid onto the appropriate finger, happy for the world to see Lorenzo's love token on her hand. When she found him alone in the *salone*, he said nothing at all for a moment as his eyes moved over her, then he seized her in his

arms and slid a hand down her spine to hold her close
against him.

"In future," he said against her mouth, "you will wear
this dress only in private with me."

"Don't you like it?"

"I like it too much," he growled. "You can feel how
much, no?"

"I can, yes!"

The sound of footsteps in the hall tore them apart, and
when Janet Shaw came in with her daughter Lorenzo was
pouring wine and Jess sitting demurely on one of the
brocade armchairs. By the time Emily and her mother
were provided with drinks cars were heard approaching
outside, and shortly afterwards Isabella, stunning in a red
dress, came rushing in with her husband, with Roberto
bringing up the rear. Andrea Moretti was neither as tall
as the Forli brothers nor as striking when it came to
looks, but Jess met humorous blue eyes in a thin, clever
face, and liked him on sight before she was engulfed in
the flood of introductions and embraces which welcomed
Lorenzo's visitors within the family circle.

Carla's dinner was a triumph, as expected. Roberto
took the seat between Emily and her mother, and flirted
so outrageously with both of them that by the time the
first course was eaten Janet Shaw had forgotten any shyness and was enjoying herself as much as her daughter.

Later, after all the toasts had been drunk, grateful
thanks expressed by the Shaws, and congratulations given
to the happy pair, Jess managed a few private words with
Isabella before the party broke up.

"Thank you so much for letting us stay at your
house!"

Isabella's eyes danced. "My little betrothal gift to you,
*cara*. I was sure you would prefer this to the hotel. And

Andrea was perfectly happy to make a surprise visit to his parents.''

Laughter dawned in Jess's eyes. "You mean—?"

"*Si*. A sudden inspiration of mine. When I suggested it to him last night Andrea, being a man, was quick to see the advantages for Lorenzo. For you, also, no?" added Isabella with a wicked little smile. "We shall leave at ten in the morning, but Lorenzo has keys to our house, so come to Lucca whenever you wish. We shall return on Sunday morning to say goodbye before you leave."

After the drive from Florence through the industry-dominated Lucchese plain, Jess was delighted with the historic centre of Lucca, where Lorenzo told her that only taxis and residents were allowed to drive within the city walls. He pointed out the Roman legacy still evident in the grid pattern of its narrow streets, and the Piazza del Mercato, which followed the shape of the original amphitheatre, then took her to the Moretti house, which was situated just within the city walls, with a small garden which backed onto the tree-crowned sixteenth-century ramparts.

"I'm so grateful to your sister for taking such trouble for us," said Jess, while Lorenzo showed her round the house.

"Since Andrea was taking his family to Siena for the night, it was no trouble. Though I, too, am grateful—*very* grateful," added Lorenzo, ushering her into the guest room.

"Andrea had no idea he was visiting his parents this weekend. At least not until Isabella informed him on Thursday after lunching at the Villa Fortuna," Jess informed him, much taken by the charm of curtains and lampshades in pomegranate silk, the dark, carved furniture.

Lorenzo began to laugh. "So. My sister took delight in playing cupid. She must like you very much, *carissima*!"

Jess turned to him with a smile. "I hope she does, but actually her main aim is to please *you*, Lorenzo."

He took her by the shoulders, sudden heat replacing the laughter in his eyes. "Is your aim the same, Jessamy. Do you wish to please me?"

Jess nodded mutely, astonished to find she felt shy now that they were alone in the room where they would sleep together for the first time. "And I'm going to start right now by putting some lunch together," she said, brisk in her effort to disguise it. "Isabella said she would leave instructions about food."

Lorenzo's eyes softened. "Have no fear, *amore*. I will not rush you straight to bed, I promise!" He put his arm round her as they went downstairs. "But I must translate Isabella's instructions for you. She speaks English very well, but to write it is beyond her."

Jess gave him a challenging look. "I hope it's not beyond you, Lorenzo, because I want lots of letters from you after I go back."

He kissed her swiftly. "I can achieve reasonable English, yes, but I trust we will not be parted long enough for me to write *very* many letters! I want you with me here as soon as possible."

In some ways feeling like a little girl playing house, Jess found it strangely exciting to prepare lunch for Lorenzo in such unexpected privacy. Lorenzo, reading from his sister's instructions, informed her that Isabella apologised for the simplicity of the food provided, but was sure Jess had better things to do than spend her time in cooking. In the refrigerator there was ravioli stuffed with spinach and cheese, ready to cook and serve with a butter sauce flavoured with fresh sage. For dinner there was *arosto misto*, which Lorenzo explained was a selection of cold roasted meat.

"Chicken, pork and spiced sausage," he reported, after inspecting a covered platter. "But we can eat out if you prefer, *carissima*."

Jess slanted a look at him. "Is that what you want to do?"

"No," he said forcibly. "I do not."

"That's settled, then, because I'd rather spend every possible minute alone here with you."

*"Grazie!"* Lorenzo made an instinctive move towards her, then halted, smiling, and threw out his hands. "See how virtuous I am!"

The flushed cook smiled at him happily, then busied herself with the unfamiliar stove, while Lorenzo sliced bread and found the butter.

"I love the bread you have here," Jess told him, when they finally began on the simple, delicious meal.

"So you will be happy to live here in my country with me?" he asked, as he poured wine.

Jess smiled. "The last two words were the important bit, Lorenzo. I just want to be wherever you are."

He reached across to take her hand. "How I wish we had met sooner, Jessamy."

She nodded. "So do I. But now we have, let's celebrate the fact." She raised her glass. "To the future."

Lorenzo echoed her toast with fervour, then in response to Jess's questions about Isabella's sons began telling her about their exploits and the devilry they got up to.

"Would you like us to have a son?" Jess asked suddenly.

Lorenzo gazed at her in eloquent silence, his eyes giving her his answer. "A son or a daughter," he said at last. "Whatever God sends, *amore*."

They cleared away together, Jess amused by Lorenzo's very obvious lack of experience in the process, and afterwards they took their coffee to drink under an umbrella outside in the small, secluded garden.

"It's lovely here, but I prefer the Villa Fortuna," said Jess, and gave him a wry little smile. "I'll tell you a little secret. I was *very* relieved when we first arrived there, Lorenzo."

His eyebrows rose. "Relieved? You found the journey from Firenze tiring?"

"No, I don't mean that." Jess looked down at her new ring, twisting it on her finger. "You house is so very different from my imaginings. I was afraid it would be horribly grand, with Venetian windows, and vast, high-ceilinged rooms full of tapestries and antique furniture so valuable I would be afraid to go anywhere near it."

Lorenzo chuckled. "The Villa Fortuna must have been a great disappointment, then. It is quite old, it is true, and large enough, but just a simple country house, Jessamy, not a Medici *palazzo*."

"Which is why I love it," she assured him. "It's so warm and welcoming. Much nicer than your apartment at the hotel."

"I shall find another apartment for us, a private one, somewhere nearby in Firenze," he promised. "I know you will not like to live in the hotel. By the time we are married I shall arrange it, *carissima*." He smiled into her eyes. "As I have said before, I would do anything in the world for you." He got to his feet. "*Allora*. Shall we take a short walk along the walls? There are good views of the city, and an occasional glimpse of a private garden like this, and when you are tired we shall stop to eat ice cream. You cannot leave Lucca without tasting some of the local *gelati*.''

Jess was delighted with the idea. The afternoon was hot, but her dark blue lawn dress was cool, and her feet were comfortable in the matching flat sandals. Lorenzo insisted she borrow a large straw hat Isabella wore in the garden, and found Jess looked so irresistible in it he promptly removed it so that he could kiss her, and Jess kissed him back, filled with a sudden desire to capture the moment and never let it go. And later, as they walked hand in hand through the double avenue of trees, she felt a fierce sense of possession when the man at her side attracted glances of open feminine admiration as they walked.

''What are you thinking, Jessamy?'' asked Lorenzo.

''You might grow conceited if I tell you,'' she said, smiling demurely.

''Are you by any chance thinking that it is good to be here with me like this?''

''Yes, I am.'' Jess smiled at him under the hat-brim. ''Do you want to know why it's so good?''

Lorenzo laughed, his grasp tightening on her hand. ''Tell me!''

''Because you belong to me. And I belong to you.''

He stopped dead to look down at her, sudden colour in his face. ''You have a habit of choosing public places to say such things, *amore*.''

They gazed at each other, oblivious of passers-by, in their absorption neither of them noticing the storm clouds beginning to gather. Suddenly it began to rain, and Lorenzo grinned, his teeth white in his dark face. He seized her hand and began to run back the way they'd come. People were running in all directions around them, there were screams as lightning flashed with a simultaneous crack of thunder, and Jess let out an excited laugh as the heavens opened in earnest, drenching them both in seconds. She ran like the wind with Lorenzo as they raced back along the ramparts, and by the time they reached the Moretti house she was panting and hot, but utterly exhilarated, her eyes glowing beneath the sodden hat-brim. Lorenzo pulled her inside and shut the door, then tossed the wrecked hat aside and pulled her into his arms to relieve her of what breath she had left by kissing her so passionately the effect of their headlong race through the storm, coupled with their utter and complete privacy in the silent house, set them both alight.

Lorenzo tore his mouth away at last and picked her up, and Jess wreathed her arms round his neck, kissing his taut, wet throat as he mounted the stairs to the guest room. The moment they were inside he set her on her feet and pulled her hard against him.

"You should have a hot bath," he panted as he drew her into the bathroom, and Jess reached behind her back for her zip with fingers too unsteady for the task.

"Help me," she said tersely, and Lorenzo spun her round, pulled the zip down and lifted her clear of the sodden dress. Jess began on Lorenzo's shirt, but he was before her, so impatient that shirt buttons went in all directions. Jess stripped herself of her wet underwear and the moment Lorenzo was equally naked he took her in his arms. Their bodies clung together, hot and wet and so taut with need that there was no more talk of a bath. Instead Lorenzo flung a large towel on the floor and they sank on it together, both of them so aroused their bodies fused without preliminaries of any kind, the savagery of the storm outside equalled by the frenzy of their love-making as they surged together towards the climax which broke over them at last like a tidal wave.

"I hurt you?" demanded Lorenzo hoarsely, when he had breath enough to speak.

Jess shook her head vehemently. "No." She heaved in a deep, quivering breath. "I had no idea it could be like that."

"I was too rough, too violent?"

"No." Jess looked up into his searching eyes, trying to find the right words. "It was—glorious!"

Lorenzo gave out a deep, relishing sigh, and pulled her up with him as he got to his feet. "I love you so much, Jessamy."

"I love you too, Signor Forli," she returned, smiling mischievously. "What shall we do now?"

"We take a shower—"

"And after that?"

The explicit gleam in Lorenzo's eyes sent shivers down her spine.

"After that, *diletta mia*, we enjoy the custom of the country. We take a siesta!"

Although they spent the major part of it in bed their time alone together passed far too quickly for Jess. She woke later that afternoon to meet Lorenzo's dark, caressing gaze, and exclaimed in dismay at wasting their time together in sleep.

"Even I," said Lorenzo modestly, "cannot make love continually, *carissima*—" He let out a howl as she gave him a very unlover-like dig in the ribs.

"I meant we could have been talking," Jess retorted, then pressed her lips and tongue on the place she'd hurt, which resulted in a very long delay before they finally went downstairs to eat the supper she was just as famished for as Lorenzo.

"This time tomorrow," said Jess, sighing, "I'll be back in London."

"Not for long," Lorenzo reminded her. "When shall I come to see your parents?"

"I'll go down next weekend. Perhaps you could come the weekend after?" Jess looked so downcast Lorenzo took her in his arms.

"You do not want me to come so soon?" he teased.

"Of course I do. But that's two whole weeks before I see you again!"

Lorenzo held her close, muttering a great many gratifying things to her, both in English and Italian. And before long they gave up any pretence of wanting to spend the evening in the Moretti *salone*, and went back upstairs to lie in each other's arms for the remainder of their time together.

By the time Isabella and Andrea arrived with their sons next morning Jess was packed and ready, dressed in the linen trousers and yellow halter top she'd worn at her first encounter with Lorenzo at the Chesterton in Pennington. There was much hugging and kissing from everyone, followed by delighted squeals of laughter as Lorenzo picked up each dark-haired little boy and spun him round, then introduced both his nephews to Jess, who was allowed a kiss from each of them.

"Thank you so much for inviting us here," said Jess later, smiling at her hosts.

"*Tante grazie*, Isabella. I am in your debt," added Lorenzo, grinning at his sister.

"Our pleasure," she assured him.

Andrea chuckled. "Once my wife ordered me to visit my parents I was most happy to oblige you, Lorenzo."

He smiled at a hectically flushed Jess. "You like our house, *cara*?"

"It's delightful," she said fervently. "It was so kind of you to give us time together like this before I go back." She pulled a face. "Something I'm not looking forward to very much."

"Nor I," said Lorenzo broodingly, then smiled as he warded off the two clamouring little boys. "*Basta*—enough! They want me to play football in the garden, Jessamy. Support me, Andrea, *per favore*. A few moments only; it grows late."

When they were alone Isabella smiled sympathetically at Jess. "You look tired, *cara*. Was the bed in my guest room not comfortable?" She clapped a hand to her mouth in distress when Jess blushed to the roots of her hair. "Forgive me—I did not mean to embarrass you. I speak before I think."

Jess laughed wryly. "The bed was very comfortable and the room is so charming we spent most of our time there."

Isabella put an arm round Jess's waist and kissed her affectionately. "I have never seen my brother look so happy and relaxed. It is so wonderful to see him like this. He looks tired," she added, eyes sparkling, "but years younger!"

Jess looked out of the window to watch Lorenzo dribbling the football down the garden like a Juventas striker, his nephews in hot pursuit. "Isabella," she said at last, "could I ask you something?"

"Anything, *cara*. What do you wish to know?"

"Would you mind telling me how Lorenzo's wife died? I don't like to ask. But I need to know just to avoid hurting him in any way."

Isabella sighed heavily, her face sombre. "I agree it is best you know, *cara*. Lorenzo never speaks of it because it is so painful to him. Poor Renata. After all those years without babies she died in childbirth."

# CHAPTER TWELVE

THE ARRIVAL of the men put an abrupt end to the conversation, for which Jess, feeling as though she'd been dealt a mortal blow, was passionately grateful. In shocked silence she shrugged into her jacket and handed her luggage over to Lorenzo to take to the car, and hoped that if anyone noticed her lack of conversation they would put it down to her sadness at the coming parting. She hugged both Andrea and Isabella wordlessly by way of thanks, received more kisses from their small sons, and soon she was on her way from Lucca on the first leg of her journey home.

"You are very quiet, *carissima*," said Lorenzo, glancing at her fleetingly as he touched her hand in sympathy.

Jess nodded mutely, somehow controlling the urge to snatch her hand away.

To her relief Lorenzo took it for granted that thoughts of leaving him had rendered her silent with misery, and because the traffic was heavy and they ran into another storm there was not only little opportunity for conversation, they were late arriving at the airport, for which Jess was fiercely grateful. Lorenzo gave her a stream of urgent instruction which needed little more than a nod of acknowledgement, then her flight was called and he seized her in his arms and held her so close she thought her ribs would break.

"Ring me at the hotel the moment you arrive at your flat," he ordered. He kissed her cold lips, then held her away a little, his eyes questioning. "What is wrong? You feel ill, *amore*?"

She nodded. "Travel nerves," she choked, desperate to get away. "I've got to go. Goodbye, Lorenzo."

Jess hurried off without looking back, knowing that a last look at Lorenzo Forli would shatter her iron control into pieces. On the plane she huddled in her window seat as the plane filled, so numb with misery she hardly noticed when the plane took off to begin its steep ascent. The couple beside her were too engrossed in each other to pay any attention to her, and Jess, grateful for it, spent the entire journey in silence, staring blankly at the blue sky above the carpet of clouds.

When she arrived at Heathrow it was almost as hot in London as Italy, and, unable to bear the idea of a train, Jess waited in line for a taxi. When she reached the flat she dumped her luggage down, switched on the water heater for a bath, then picked up the telephone and got through to the hotel beside the Arno to ask for Signor Forli.

Lorenzo answered at once, his relief evident in his tone as Jess told him she was home.

"How are you feeling, Jessamy?" he asked urgently. "I have been mad with worry. You looked so ill when you left me—"

"You know I hate flying," she cut in. "And I still feel horribly sick. I really can't talk now, Lorenzo."

"*Poverina!* I will ring you later."

"Tomorrow, *please*!" Jess implored, suddenly at the end of her tether. "I'm going straight to bed now."

When she put the phone down she realised she was still wearing Lorenzo's ring. With an exclamation of disgust she wrenched it off her shaking hand and threw it across the room, then put the kettle on and made herself a cup of black coffee to drink while she rang Friars Wood to announce her arrival. Her mother answered, and, always alert to nuances of expression when it came to her young, demanded to know what was wrong. Jess pleaded travel sickness and fatigue, reported that Emily was on the mend, and promised to ring next day after her return from the agency.

"Should you be going to work tomorrow if you feel ill, darling?"

It was preferable to staring at the walls in the flat. "I'll be fine, Mother," said Jess firmly. "I really can't take any more time off." She asked after her siblings, sent her love to her father, then put the phone down before she could weaken and sob out her sorry tale to her perceptive parent.

Once she'd showered Jess slid into bed and stared at the ceiling of the small, functional bedroom which was so different from the room she'd slept in—or not slept in—the night before. And at last the numbing fog fell away, and a great wave of anguish and disillusion swept over her.

When the storm of weeping was over Jess mopped herself up and faced facts. Just like the other men in her life, in the end Lorenzo Forli had used all the means he possessed to seduce her into his bed. Admittedly his approach had been very different from the others. Not only fairy stories about love at first sight, but shameless lies about his relationship with Renata. A novel spin on the old 'my wife doesn't understand me' gambit, thought Jess, and ground her teeth in furious distaste. She had been so gullible, so full of compassion for him as Lorenzo had told her about his arid, loveless marriage. She'd listened with such sympathy, aching for him when he said he had never touched Renata again after their

wedding night. Yet the inescapable truth remained. To
die in childbirth Renata had to have been pregnant first.
Which meant that at a late stage in the relationship either
Lorenzo had resorted to force or Renata had experienced
some kind of epiphany and welcomed him into her bed
at last.

The thought acted on Jess like an emetic, and she
bolted to the bathroom, her fiction about nausea suddenly
the truth. Later she lay awake for hours in shivering misery, bitter as she remembered the way Roberto and
Isabella had pleaded with her not to hurt Lorenzo. Jess
buried her face in the pillow. In the end *she* was the one
who'd been hurt, not their beloved brother. And the worst
of it was she still loved Lorenzo passionately, and wanted
him here right now, in this bed beside her. She groaned
in despair, mortified by her own weakness. In the past
she'd been so scornful about sensible friends who
changed overnight into mooning idiots over men. She had
sworn it would never happen to Jess Dysart. Yet here she
was, for the first time in her life helplessly, hopelessly in
love. So much so she'd surrendered unconditionally to
the man who'd taught her just how breathtakingly wonderful love could be. Only to discover that the object of
her passion was not nearly as perfect as she—and everyone else who knew him—believed. Lorenzo Forli was as
capable of lying to gain his ends as any lesser mortal.

At some time in the night Jess fell into a troubled
sleep, but woke early to crawl out of bed and search the
floor on hands and knees until she found the ring. She
sat down at once to write a cool, dignified letter to
Lorenzo, telling him that their brief, passionate relationship had been a mistake. Too hot not to cool down and
all that. Not that this was true. She hadn't cooled down.
The merest thought of Lorenzo's lips and hands… Jess

groaned in anguish and went to stand under the shower again.

Her first day back at the agency was an unwelcome revelation to Jess. She had counted on using work as an opiate for the injury to her damaged heart. But to her consternation she found she no longer had any enthusiasm for her job. The work she had once found so interesting now seemed trivial and boring. And without Emily to come home to in the evening the small basement flat felt like a stuffy prison after the space and charm of Villa Fortuna.

Jess worked late that first, endless day, and returned home eventually to listen to several messages from Lorenzo demanding that she ring him back. Refusing to add expensive phone calls to the bill she shared with Emily, Jess took a shower, made a sandwich with the groceries she'd bought on the way home, then sat down with it to wait.

Before she was even half way through her sandwich Lorenzo rang again.

"You are there!" he said with relief when she answered. "I was so worried, *amore*. Where have you been?"

"Working. I had a lot of catching up to do."

"I hate to think of you working so hard. Do you feel better? he demanded.

"It all depends on what you mean by better."

"You are saying you miss me," he said, the triumphant note in his voice acting like a match on the fuse of her anger. "*Carissima*, I know how you feel. I miss you so very much already—"

"I'm afraid," she said coldly, "you'll have to get used to that, Lorenzo. And you have no idea how I feel."

"*Cosa?*" he said incredulously. There was a pause. "What do you mean?"

"I mean," said Jess with deliberate cruelty, "that I won't be seeing you again."

"What is this nonsense?" he demanded roughly. "You are saying you no longer want me?"

If she did she'd be lying. Jess gritted her teeth. "Let's just say I no longer want to marry you. It was a crazy idea anyway. I've written a letter to explain. You should receive it shortly—"

"Jessamy!" he said urgently. "What has happened? What has changed your mind? I cannot believe you mean this, not after the joy we shared—"

"You mean sex," she said scornfully. "Don't worry, Lorenzo. I'm sure you'll soon find another woman just as gullible as me, only too happy to pander to your needs. Goodbye."

Jess put the phone down and threw herself on the sofa, sobbing bitterly. As expected the phone rang again soon afterwards, and with clenched fists rammed against her quivering mouth she listened to Lorenzo's enraged voice ordering her to pick up the phone. Eventually, when it became clear to him she had no intention of obeying him, he rang off. Soon afterwards the phone rang again, but this time Frances Dysart's voice began leaving a message, and Jess picked up the receiver to assure her mother she was feeling better, though her first day at work had been hard going.

"You don't sound better. Are you coming down this weekend?" asked Frances. "We'd love to hear all about Lorenzo's home. Your father was very taken with him, darling. Are you seeing him again?"

"No," said Jess flatly. "I'm not."

There was a pause. "Something wrong?"

"No, not really." Jess managed a laugh. "Lorenzo's quite a charmer, I grant you. But not really my type."

"If you say so."

"I do. Have you heard from the honeymooners?"

Taking this as a plea for less emotive conversation, Frances gave news of Leo and Jonah, who were returning shortly, Kate, who had finished her exams, Adam, who was still awaiting the results of his, and Fenella, who had quarrelled with her best friend. Soothed by the minutiae of life at Friars Wood, Jess promised to travel down the following Saturday and returned to her sandwich. But, revolted by it, and every other form of food, she threw it away and made herself some tea, then tried to watch some television. But the programme could have been broadcast in Sanskrit for all the sense she made of it, as she sat waiting for the phone to ring again.

When it did, a long, endless hour later, Jess waited for Lorenzo's voice to start making demands again, but instead it was Emily, sounding very distressed, and Jess seized the phone to answer her.

"What's up, love?" she said breathlessly.

"You're asking *me* that?" said Emily, incensed. "What the devil are you playing at, Jess Dysart?"

"What do you mean?"

"What do I mean! Lorenzo drove here a short while ago, asking if I'd heard from you. And behind that controlled mask of his he was in a terrible state. When I said I hadn't spoken to you since you went back he apologised for disturbing Mother and me, and took off again. What's going on?"

"I've told him I don't want to see him again."

*"What?"* Emily said something her mother would have been horrified to hear. "Well, that's a lie for a start. Whatever happened to truly, madly, deeply?"

Jess sighed wearily. "I was given certain information about his past. Something I just can't cope with."

"Are you sure about this? Whoever told you could have got it wrong."

"Not likely. It was Isabella."

Emily breathed in sharply, then began to cough, and it was some time before she was able to speak again. "Sorry about that. Look, I must ring off. This is costing Lorenzo a fortune, and heaven knows he's shelled out enough already. On both of us," she added. "Look, Jess, are you sure you haven't got the wrong end of the stick somehow?"

"Very sure," said Jess desolately. "I wish I had."

As the week dragged on there were no more calls from Lorenzo. Which came as a mortifying surprise. Jess had been so sure he would persist until he knew the reason for her attitude. She had looked forward to throwing the truth in his face, daring him to deny that Renata had lost her life trying to give birth to his child. In her stilted, brief letter, which had taken sheet after sheet of rough drafts before she was satisfied, she'd said nothing about Renata. She wrote that it had been a mistake to agree to marry him after so short an acquaintance, and therefore she was returning the ring.

After years of trying to diet herself into something approaching her sisters' slenderness Jess found her weight diminishing by the day. Which was no surprise. Since her return from Italy the mere thought of food had sickened her. Lorenzo Forli was to blame, she thought in anguish. At last Jess gave up expecting a message from him whenever she got home, but couldn't control a wild leap of hope every time the phone rang, just the same. On one occasion it was Simon Hollister, her fellow juror, who rang up as he'd promised, suggesting a meal. Why not? thought Jess wearily, but arranged to meet him for a drink instead of putting him to the expense of food she couldn't eat. Simon was an amusing companion, and the evening passed pleasantly enough, but when he suggested a repeat Jess was vague, saying she'd give him a ring when she was free. Simon was nice. But he wasn't Lorenzo. No one was. Nor ever would be.

Lack of nutrition, sleep, and enthusiasm for life in general, made Jess very tired as the week wore on. After coping with the tantrums of a model whose success had gone to her undeniably beautiful head, she was late getting back to the flat on Friday evening, and when the doorbell rang soon afterwards she groaned in despair, in no mood to talk to anyone.

"Mr and Mrs Savage here, Jess," said her sister's voice over the intercom. "Let us in."

Leonie rushed in through the door Jess opened and gave her sister a hug, then stood back, eyeing her in frank, sisterly horror. "Good heavens above, Jess, what have you done to yourself?"

"Thanks!" said Jess dryly, then submitted herself to Jonah's embrace in turn. "Go on," she told him, resigned. "Get your bit over with as well. I know I look gruesome."

Like his wife, Jonah Savage looked the picture of health and happiness, but his eyes were full of concern. "Never gruesome, love," he assured her, "but something's obviously wrong, Jess. What's up? Your mother told us to come round and check on you the moment we reached London."

Leonie gave her husband a speaking look. "Pop out and buy some wine, darling. I think a drink is called for."

"I've got some wine," protested Jess.

"My beloved means she wants me to make myself scarce for a bit," said Jonah, grinning. "Though by the look of her, Leo, Jess could do with a double helping of fish and chips, not wine."

Jess shuddered, clapped a hand over her mouth and fled to the bathroom. When she emerged, ashen and shivering, Jonah had vanished and his bride was making tea.

"Better?" asked Leonie. "Come and sit down. Mother told me all about Emily and your mercy trip to Florence with Lorenzo, not to mention the stay at the Villa Fortuna. I gather you and Lorenzo hit it off to such an extent Mother can't understand why you don't want to see him any more. What went wrong?"

"Oh, you know me and men, Leo," said Jess flippantly. "I never get it right."

"Hmm." Leonie added milk to the steaming beakers and handed one to Jess. "Kate assured me that you and Lorenzo are—I quote—'madly in love'."

Jess scowled. "We hardly know each other."

"What difference does that make? I knew Jonah was the man for me the moment I met him."

"That's different."

"Why?"

"Jonah's a straight arrow."

"And Lorenzo isn't?" Leonie frowned. "Strange. Roberto—who is nobody's fool, Jess—has enormous respect for him."

"I don't want to talk about it," said Jess mulishly, then rushed off to throw up again, which was a painful process on an empty stomach. When she got back to the sitting room Leonie fixed her with a searching dark eye.

"Look, love, you're not—not in the same boat as me by any chance, are you?"

Jess flushed painfully. "No, I'm not," she said miserably, and burst into tears.

Leonie took her in her arms and let her cry for some time. At last Jess mastered herself and sat up, scrubbing at her eyes.

"For your ears only, I suppose I could have been pregnant," she admitted reluctantly. "But today I found I wasn't."

"But you wish you were!"

"Even if I was," flared Jess, "I wouldn't tell him."

"By 'him' I assume you mean Lorenzo Forli?"

"Of course I do."

"Mystery solved, then. You're throwing up because you're heartbroken. I remember the quarrel you had with some boy after a school dance," Leonie reminded her. "You were sick for days afterwards."

"Right." Jess pulled a face. "But this is in a different class from that, unfortunately. I can't eat, can't sleep, hate my job, and if this is love you can stuff it!"

Leonie smiled sympathetically. "I know how you feel. I've been there myself. But don't punish yourself if you do want Lorenzo, Jess. Life's too short. What on earth did he do to get you in this state?"

"He lied to me, Leo."

Leonie stared in astonishment. "Is that all? Haven't you ever lied to anyone?"

"Not about something as serious as this."

Leonie sighed, then got up as the doorbell rang. "That'll be Jonah."

Jonah, to Jess's relief, had not carried out his threat about fish and chips. Instead he presented her with a six-pack of mineral water and ordered her to eat something before she wasted away. Then Leonie, well aware that Jess needed to be alone, announced it was time to go.

"Jess, we're off to eat with my parents now," said Jonah as they left. "But we're going down to Friars Wood in time for dinner tomorrow night."

"I'll see you tomorrow, then," said Jess, smiling valiantly.

Leonie gave her a rather protracted hug, and smoothed the damp hair back from her sister's forehead. "Think about what I said," she instructed, and nodded towards the telephone. "Call him."

"Call who?" demanded Jonah.

"Tell you on the way home," promised Leonie, then smiled at Jess. "And tomorrow we'll bore you with tales of our stay in France."

Jess bit her lip in remorse. "Sorry! I forgot to ask how you enjoyed your honeymoon." She managed a smile. "Not that I need to. You both look wonderful."

When she was alone Jess sat staring at the telephone, wondering whether to follow her sister's advice. But it rang before she could make up her mind. To her disappointment it was Emily, saying she was flying back in the morning and would be staying with her mother until their own doctor pronounced her fit to return to work.

"How are you feeling?" asked Jess.

"Still a bit feeble, but definitely on the mend. I'm enormously grateful to Lorenzo," added Emily deliberately, "for providing me with such a marvellous place to convalesce in. And for inviting my mother here as the icing on the cake. It's been a great treat for her."

Jess fought with herself and lost. "Have you seen him?" she asked gruffly.

"Of course I've seen him. He looks terrible."

"Easy to see whose side you're on," said Jess bitterly.

"Must there be sides? I just want to see you both happy again, like you were before. Anyway," Emily went on quickly, "for heaven's sake don't wallow in gloom all weekend in the flat, Jess."

"Of course I won't! I'm off home to Friars Wood in the morning."

The conversation with Emily decided Jess to ring Lorenzo next day, and at least let him know her reason for ending things between them. Her empty stomach reacted to the sense of the decision by demanding food, and Jess made herself some toast, took it to bed with a mug of tea, and once she'd consumed her little feast fell fast asleep. She surfaced so late next morning it was time to drive immediately to Stavely, if she had any hope of arriving at Friars Wood for lunch. The phone call to Lorenzo was too important to be rushed, Jess decided. She would ring him when she got home.

The hot weather had broken, and the trip along the motorway was punctuated by heavy showers which made driving difficult. By the time the car was buffeted about by crosswinds on the Severn Bridge Jess was heartily glad she was almost home. The main door of Friars Wood opened the minute her car reached the terrace, and all four Dysarts in residence came rushing out with the dog to welcome her back.

"Adam's still in Edinburgh," said Frances Dysart over lunch. "Mrs Briggs is coming in later, to clean bathrooms and help with dinner and so on. Why not have a rest in Adam's bed in the Stables this afternoon, Jess?"

"Good idea!" Jess smiled brightly, secretly glad at the prospect as she helped herself to a modest portion of chicken salad.

"You've lost weight," accused her father, now he'd had time to look at her properly. "Didn't you eat anything in Italy?"

"Of course I did. The food was wonderful. But I've

been very busy since I got back.'' Jess kept the smile pinned on her face. ''I soon worked the extra pounds off.''

''And a few more while you were at it,'' said Kate with sibling bluntness.

''Is Lorenzo's house nice, Jess?'' asked Fenny eagerly.

''Yes,'' said Jess casually, breaking an awkward little silence. ''It's lovely. Right out in the countryside. My friend Emily soon got better once she arrived there.''

''How is Emily?'' said Frances quickly, to stave off more questions from Fenny.

''Much better. She should be home by now; she was flying back with her mother this morning.''

After the strain of keeping a brave face in front of her family Jess was tired, and grateful to her mother for the unexpected privacy of the Stables. Once she'd had some coffee after the meal she smiled apologetically, and said she was off to Adam's bed.

''Pathetic, I know, but it was a nasty drive down, and I'm really tired. I promise I'll be more lively by the time the others arrive.''

''I'll help you carry your things,'' said Kate.

Adam's room in the Stables was furnished entirely to his own taste, with a vast brass bed and tawny orange walls, and to Jess it felt like a warm, welcoming haven. Kate dumped her sister's holdall on the floor and took a change of clothes out of it, but made no attempt to ask questions Jess wasn't ready to answer.

''Get your things off and pop straight into bed,'' said Kate. ''I'll take your holdall back and hang the rest of your stuff in your own room. Mother's put milk and things in the fridge downstairs, so you can make yourself some tea when you get up. In the meantime we shall all be frightfully tactful and refrain from asking what happened to make you look so—''

''Ghastly?''

''I was going to say fragile,'' said Kate, looking worried.

''Sounds good. No one's ever called me fragile before,'' added Jess with a genuine chuckle. ''How did the exams go?''

''All right, I think.''

''Which means brilliantly, of course, Miss Genius.''

Kate grimaced and crossed her fingers. ''Don't tempt fate, please!''

When Jess was alone she stretched out in the big bed, deciding to ring Lorenzo later. Right now she just couldn't face it. All she wanted to do was sleep and sleep, and wake up to find herself back at the moment before Isabella Moretti had innocently put an end to the fairy tale.

When Jess woke rain was lashing against the windows. As usual, ever since her flight from Italy, the first waking moment was the worst, but Jess lay quiet, weathering the pain as she tried to think of what to say if—when—she rang Lorenzo. Here at home she was her rational self again, with the courage to face the truth. She loved Lorenzo whether he'd lied or not.

Jess listened suddenly, aware that someone was in the house.

''Is that you, Kate?'' she called. She jumped out of bed and pulled on Adam's bathrobe, and went to the door, yawning. ''If so you can make some tea.'' She peered over the banisters on the small landing and looked down for a long, frozen moment into Lorenzo's haggard, upturned face. His hair was wet, and his eyes held a look which pierced Jess to the heart.

"Forgive if I startled you, Jessamy. Kate insisted I wait alone until you wake," said Lorenzo, his English less polished than usual.

"How—why are you here?" said Jess with difficulty.

"I flew to England last night. I stay at the Chesterton again." Lorenzo thrust a hand through his wet hair, his bleak, bloodshot eyes holding hers. "Please dress and come down. I wish to talk to you, Jessamy. After that—" He stopped, his mouth twisting. "After that, if you no longer desire my company I shall return to Firenze."

Jess looked at him for a long moment, then nodded. "Just give me five minutes."

"*Grazie,*" he said tonelessly, and turned away.

Jess dressed at top speed in a faded pink sweatshirt and old jeans grown soft with washing, then went downstairs to Adam's sitting room. Lorenzo was standing in front of the fireplace, dressed informally in a blue chambray shirt and jeans very much like hers, though Jess had no doubt they bore a more exalted label. But he wore beautiful leather shoes, as usual, and a rain-marked suede jacket lay on the back of a chair.

"You look tired, Jessamy," he said quietly.

"So do you."

He nodded. "I have slept very little since you left. Even less after I received your letter."

She looked away, not ready, yet, to get to the heart of the matter. "You must be cold. Can I make you some coffee?"

"*Grazie.*"

Jess went through to the kitchen to fill Adam's kettle, and Lorenzo followed her, watching silently while she spooned instant coffee into beakers and set out milk and sugar.

"How did you know I'd be here at Friars Wood?" she asked quietly.

"I rang your parents when I arrived."

She looked up in surprise. "They didn't tell me!"

He nodded soberly. "I requested their silence. I feared that if you knew I was here you would refuse to speak to me." He paused, but Jess remained silent, her eyes fixed on his. "Jessamy," he said at last, "you would give me no reason for your change of heart, but I have now discovered this."

So not much point in hurling accusations after all. Not that she wanted to any more, now they were face to face. "What exactly did you discover?" Jess asked gruffly, needing to establish the facts.

"Eventually I found that my sister told you how Renata died," said Lorenzo flatly.

Jess handed him a mug of coffee, then led the way back to the other room. Lorenzo followed her to the large chesterfield sofa, waited until Jess curled up in one corner, then seated himself at the other end to sit staring into the empty fireplace. And at last the silence between them grew so tense Jess could bear it no longer.

"If things had continued as planned. Before Isabella told me, I mean," she said carefully, "had you any intention of telling me the truth at some time?"

"Yes. Though the truth was not really mine to tell." Lorenzo set the mug down on a small table beside him, then turned weary eyes on her. "I have never lied to you, Jessamy."

"How do you expect me to believe that?" she demanded. "You told me you had never lived a normal married life with Renata. Yet she died in childbirth."

Lorenzo's jaw tightened. "This is true. I received

much sympathy, many, many condolences. They sickened me."

Jess eyed him narrowly. "But in the circumstances surely it would have been odd if you'd received no sympathy at all, Lorenzo?"

"I would have preferred that," he said with force. "But how could I tell my family, my friends, that for the last few months of my marriage I had been forced to live an even greater lie than in all the years before? Roberto, Isabella, neither of them knew the truth. I have never told anyone until now." He met her eyes. "I was not the father of Renata's child."

"Lorenzo!" Jess stared at him in horror, then slid along the couch to take his hand. "You mean she had a *lover*?"

Lorenzo looked down at the hand grasping his. "I thought I would never feel your touch again," he said unevenly.

Jess's self-control, which had been notable by its absence since her return from Italy, abruptly deserted her. Tears streamed down her face, and with a smothered exclamation Lorenzo put his arms round her and held her close.

"*Piangi!*" he commanded, smoothing her head against his shoulder, and Jess obeyed, letting the hot, salt tears wash away the misery of their parting.

"Sorry," she said thickly at last, and pulled away to fish in her pocket for the tissues she was lately never without. "I've cried more this last week than in my entire life." She smiled up at him damply, and almost started crying again when she saw a trace of moisture on Lorenzo's thick black lashes.

"I have been in torment," he said roughly. "I had even begun to wish we had never met."

Jess managed a smile. "I never got as far as that. But—"

"But what, *amore*?" he whispered.

"Even if we'd never met again I couldn't be sorry that you'd made love to me, Lorenzo."

"To hear you say this—" He let out a deep, shaky breath. "You know that I have only to touch you to want to make love to you again, but it is not for this that I am here."

"You don't want to make love to me?"

Lorenzo tapped a reproving forefinger against her flushed cheek. "You know very well that I do. That I always will while there is breath in my body. But first we must talk, to remove this cloud from our lives."

"If you don't want to tell me about Renata I don't mind," said Jess quickly. "Now I know the truth we can never talk about it again, if you prefer."

Lorenzo shook his head vehemently. "I swore to her that I would never reveal her secret, but I feel a deep need to talk to *you*, Jessamy. To tell you what no other living person knows about my life. I want no secrets between us, *carissima*." He drew in a deep breath. "Renata begged me to pose as father of her child."

Jess breathed in sharply. "She asked too much of you, Lorenzo. What happened? Did Renata just fall in love with someone else?"

"When Renata was forced, at last, to tell me what happened," began Lorenzo, his arm tightening round Jess, "she was hysterical with shame, and—and incoherent. That is right?"

Jess nodded. "As well she might be." She looked up in sudden fear. "Don't tell me she was raped!"

"*Dio*, no," said Lorenzo swiftly. "Not that." His mouth twisted. "Though in some ways I believe she would have actually preferred this, so that the guilt was not hers.''

Renata, he began slowly, had been in the habit of staying for long periods in her family's country home near Perugia. Lorenzo had been grateful for solitude in the house in Oltrarno, and Renata, never suited to matrimony, had been happy to stay for weeks at a time with her widowed mother. When her mother died Renata had inherited the house and spent even more time there.

One summer, while the housekeeper was on holiday, Renata had been alone in the house during one of the violent storms which had always terrified her. The man who took care of the garden had just left, and when the bell rang at the gate Renata, thinking it was the old gardener, returning to shelter from the storm, had run through the rain to let him in, desperate for company. Instead of the gardener she had found a drenched young man with a backpack asking for shelter until the storm passed.

Jess moved closer. "What happened then?"

"Renata grew even more hysterical at this point," said Lorenzo tonelessly. "Eventually I learned that the man was a foreign tourist, young, and very beautiful, with long golden hair like an angel, she told me. Fortunately for Renata, who was no linguist, he spoke a little Italian. When the storm grew fiercer he asked to stay the night. She agreed, and gave him wine and food." His mouth twisted. "She even gave him dry clothes that I had left there once."

"So he was tall, this stranger," said Jess thoughtfully.

Lorenzo shrugged. "More important than that, Renata confessed that for the first time in her life she was physically attracted to a man—"

"Even though she was married to you?" said Jess fiercely, and clutched his hand. "She was a fool!"

"Thank you, *carissima*. You are very good for my self-esteem." Lorenzo gave her a fleeting smile. "To end the story, in the night lightning struck a tree in the garden. Renata screamed, the stranger rushed to see what was wrong, and the rest you can imagine."

"How on earth did you feel when she told you that?" said Jess, outraged.

Lorenzo shrugged graphically. "I have no English words to describe this. I cared nothing that she had taken a lover at last. But I cursed the man who went on his way next morning without a thought for the woman who spent most of her life afterwards on her knees in penitence. Renata looked on the pregnancy as punishment for her sin. This must sound dramatic to you, I know well, but all her life she had been very devout. Her guilt was so great she lost the will to live." Lorenzo's arm tightened. "She would not eat, could not sleep, and spent hours every day in prayer. The result was inevitable. When Renata gave birth, months too early, she died with her child."

Jess shuddered, and held Lorenzo close. "I was such a fool," she said bitterly.

He turned her face up to his. "A fool, *innamorata*? Why?"

"Because I didn't trust you." Her eyes blazed into his beneath their swollen lids. "I once gave Leo a lecture for failing to trust Jonah, but I was no better where you're concerned. When Isabella told me how Renata died I should have confronted you with it right away. But my blind instinct was to run as far away from you as I could get." She smiled shakily. "I was so disillusioned, Lorenzo. To me you were unique. Not only because I was madly in love with you, but for being such a saint where Renata was concerned—''

''I am no saint,'' he said harshly, and pulled her close, his eyes boring into hers. ''But I did not lie to you, Jessamy. And I never will. *Sempre la verità*, I promised. And I meant it.''

Jess flung her arms round his neck and kissed him with passionate remorse. Lorenzo's response was everything she'd dreamed of in the long, unbearable days since she'd left him. At last he held her away a little, breathing rapidly.

''Since you left me I suffered torment for another reason, also.''

''Why?''

Lorenzo took her face in his hands. ''I desired you so much I did not take the necessary care. I feared you might be expecting my child and would never tell me.''

She shook her head. ''I'm not.''

He sighed heavily. ''In one way I hoped so much that you were.''

Jess smiled a little. ''So did I.''

Lorenzo's answering smile transformed his face so completely she was dazzled. ''You mean this?''

She nodded. ''When I had time to think, alone in the flat, I realised that even if you weren't the prince in my fairy tale, but just a normal, mortal man after all, I still loved you, Lorenzo. Just like all the Dysart females I'm a one-man woman, it seems.'' Her mouth drooped. ''I was heartbroken when I found I wasn't pregnant.''

Lorenzo's English deserted him completely. He held her close, saying a great many things that Jess needed no interpreter to translate, but eventually, with mutual reluctance, they agreed it was time to go over to the house.

''Before another minute passes,'' said Lorenzo, ''I

must ask your parents' approval. Do you think they will agree to give me their daughter?''

Later that evening, when the newlyweds arrived, Leonie exclaimed in delight when she found Lorenzo with Jess, and after drinks had been served to mark the homecoming of the bride and groom the family gathered round the dining table for the celebration dinner Kate had been helping her mother prepare for most of the day.

Fenny, in all the glory of her bridesmaid dress, was allowed to stay up for dinner, and asked Lorenzo endless questions about his house, then turned on Jonah with equally relentless curiosity to ask when the baby would come.

''Fenella!'' said Frances in dismay.

''People always have babies when they get married,'' said Fenny, undeterred. ''My friend Laura told me.''

''Then of course it must be true,'' said Tom Dysart, chuckling, and smiled apologetically at Jonah. ''Sorry about that.''

''No problem,'' said Leonie, exchanging a glance with her jubilant bridegroom. ''Actually, we think about Christmas time, Fen.''

Jess felt Lorenzo's hand tighten on hers under the table, and smiled to herself.

Kate stared at the blushing bride in surprise. ''Which Christmas?'' she demanded.

''This one,'' said Jonah smugly.

Fenny frowned in disappointment. ''That's a long time yet.'' She stared, puzzled, as everyone laughed, and Jess relaxed, aware that her parents, at least, had known before the general announcement.

''You knew this?'' asked Lorenzo.

Jess nodded. ''You should be grateful for it, too.''

"I?" he demanded.

"If Leo hadn't wept all over me and confessed she was pregnant I wouldn't have come rushing to Pennington that night to collect her earrings."

"Then you are right," said Lorenzo fervently. "I am *very* grateful."

When the meal was over, and they were still sitting round the table over coffee, Tom Dysart opened two bottles of champagne and with Jonah's help refilled all the glasses. Then he held up his hand for silence, smiling at the expectant faces turned towards him. "This seems to be a night for important announcements! I'm sure everyone here will be happy to know that earlier today Lorenzo asked our permission to marry Jess. He doesn't need it, of course, but both Frances and I were very happy to give them our blessing." He raised his glass. "To Jess and Lorenzo."

After the expected rush of kisses and congratulations Lorenzo Forli, looking very different from the dishevelled, wild-eyed man Jess had found earlier in the Stables, stood up, his face eloquent with such happiness and pride Jess felt a great tide of love rise inside her as he replied to the toast.

"I am very grateful to all of you for your kindness and good wishes," he began, and smiled down at Jess. "I know it is a very short time since I met Jessamy, but I wanted her for my wife from the first moment I met her, and promise to take great care of her. I consider myself the most fortunate man alive to have won her love."

There was much applause and excitement, and eventually Kate elected to haul an excited Fenny off to bed.

"Can I be bridesmaid, Jess?" Fenny demanded as she kissed her goodnight.

"I'm counting on it!"

"Let's get that dress off, then," said Kate, laughing. "You may need it again."

Later, when they were all gathered in the drawing room, Leonie left her place by Jonah to join Lorenzo and Jess on the sofa they were sharing.

"I'm the only one in the family who has the least idea how things were for you in the past, Lorenzo," she said in an undertone. "This time I know you'll be happy."

"I cannot fail to be with Jessamy for my wife," he said with certainty. "You know from Roberto that life has not always been good for me, but all that is in the past, Leonie. The moment I met your sister my life changed."

"For the better, I hope," teased Jess, smiling up at him.

"You know this very well." Lorenzo kissed her swiftly, oblivious of indulgent onlookers. "As I have told you often before, *innamorata*, you are my reward!"

*Harlequin truly does make any time special. ...
This year we are celebrating weddings in style!*

A Walk Down the Aisle
WEDDING CELEBRATION

To help us celebrate, we want you to tell us how wearing the Harlequin wedding gown will make your wedding day special. As the grand prize, Harlequin will offer one lucky bride the chance to **"Walk Down the Aisle" in the Harlequin wedding gown!**

### There's more...

For her honeymoon, she and her groom will spend five nights at the **Hyatt Regency Maui.** As part of this five-night honeymoon at the hotel renowned for its romantic attractions, the couple will enjoy a candlelit dinner for two in Swan Court, a sunset sail on the hotel's catamaran, and duet spa treatments.

Maui • Molokai • Lanai

To enter, please write, in, 250 words or less, how wearing the Harlequin wedding gown will make your wedding day special. The entry will be judged based on its emotionally compelling nature, its originality and creativity, and its sincerity. This contest is open to Canadian and U.S. residents only and to those who are 18 years of age and older. There is no purchase necessary to enter. Void where prohibited. See further contest rules attached. Please send your entry to:

### Walk Down the Aisle Contest

| In Canada | In U.S.A. |
|---|---|
| P.O. Box 637 | P.O. Box 9076 |
| Fort Erie, Ontario | 3010 Walden Ave. |
| L2A 5X3 | Buffalo, NY 14269-9076 |

You can also enter by visiting www.eHarlequin.com
***Win the Harlequin wedding gown and the vacation of a lifetime!***
The deadline for entries is October 1, 2001.

HARLEQUIN®
*Makes any time special* ®

PHWDACONT1

HARLEQUIN WALK DOWN THE AISLE TO MAUI CONTEST 1197
OFFICIAL RULES
NO PURCHASE NECESSARY TO ENTER

1. To enter, follow directions published in the offer to which you are responding. Contest begins April 2, 2001, and ends on October 1, 2001. Method of entry may vary. Mailed entries must be postmarked by October 1, 2001, and received by October 8, 2001.

2. Contest entry may be, at times, presented via the Internet, but will be restricted solely to residents of certain geographic areas that are disclosed on the Web site. To enter via the Internet, if permissible, access the Harlequin Web site (www.eHarlequin.com) and follow the directions displayed online. Online entries must be received by 11:59 p.m. E.S.T. on October 1, 2001.

   In lieu of submitting an entry online, enter by mail by hand-printing (or typing) on an 8½" x 11" plain piece of paper, your name, address (including zip code), Contest number/name and in 250 words or fewer, why winning a Harlequin wedding dress would make your wedding day special. Mail via first-class mail to: Harlequin Walk Down the Aisle Contest 1197, (in the U.S.) P.O. Box 9076, 3010 Walden Avenue, Buffalo, NY 14269-9076, (in Canada) P.O. Box 637, Fort Erie, Ontario L2A 5X3, Canada.

   Limit one entry per person, household address and e-mail address. Online and/or mailed entries received from persons residing in geographic areas in which Internet entry is not permissible will be disqualified.

3. Contests will be judged by a panel of members of the Harlequin editorial, marketing and public relations staff based on the following criteria:

   - Originality and Creativity—50%
   - Emotionally Compelling—25%
   - Sincerity—25%

   In the event of a tie, duplicate prizes will be awarded. Decisions of the judges are final.

4. All entries become the property of Torstar Corp. and will not be returned. No responsibility is assumed for lost, late, illegible, incomplete, inaccurate, nondelivered or misdirected mail or misdirected e-mail, or for technical, hardware or software failures of any kind, lost or unavailable network connections, or failed, incomplete, garbled or delayed computer transmission or any human error which may occur in the receipt or processing of the entries in this Contest.

5. Contest open only to residents of the U.S. (except Puerto Rico) and Canada, who are 18 years of age or older, and is void where prohibited by law; all applicable laws and regulations apply. Any litigation within the Province of Quebec respecting the conduct or organization of a publicity contest may be submitted to the Régie des alcools, des courses et des jeux for a ruling. Any litigation respecting the awarding of a prize may be submitted to the Régie des alcools, des courses et des jeux only for the purpose of helping the parties reach a settlement. Employees and immediate family members of Torstar Corp. and D. L. Blair, Inc., their affiliates, subsidiaries and all other agencies, entities and persons connected with the use, marketing or conduct of this Contest are not eligible to enter. Taxes on prizes are the sole responsibility of winners. Acceptance of any prize offered constitutes permission to use winner's name, photograph or other likeness for the purposes of advertising, trade and promotion on behalf of Torstar Corp., its affiliates and subsidiaries without further compensation to the winner, unless prohibited by law.

6. Winners will be determined no later than November 15, 2001, and will be notified by mail. Winners will be required to sign and return an Affidavit of Eligibility form within 15 days after winner notification. Noncompliance within that time period may result in disqualification and an alternative winner may be selected. Winners of trip must execute a Release of Liability prior to ticketing and must possess required travel documents (e.g. passport, photo ID) where applicable. Trip must be completed by November 2002. No substitution of prize permitted by winner. Torstar Corp. and D. L. Blair, Inc., their parents, affiliates, and subsidiaries are not responsible for errors in printing or electronic presentation of Contest, entries and/or game pieces. In the event of printing or other errors which may result in unintended prize values or duplication of prizes, all affected game pieces or entries shall be null and void. If for any reason the Internet portion of the Contest is not capable of running as planned, including infection by computer virus, bugs, tampering, unauthorized intervention, fraud, technical failures, or any other causes beyond the control of Torstar Corp. which corrupt or affect the administration, secrecy, fairness, integrity or proper conduct of the Contest, Torstar Corp. reserves the right, at its sole discretion, to disqualify any individual who tampers with the entry process and to cancel, terminate, modify or suspend the Contest or the Internet portion thereof. In the event of a dispute regarding an online entry, the entry will be deemed submitted by the authorized holder of the e-mail account submitted at the time of entry. Authorized account holder is defined as the natural person who is assigned to an e-mail address by an Internet access provider, online service provider or other organization that is responsible for arranging e-mail address for the domain associated with the submitted e-mail address. **Purchase or acceptance of a product offer does not improve your chances of winning.**

7. Prizes: (1) Grand Prize—A Harlequin wedding dress (approximate retail value: $3,500) and a 5-night/6-day honeymoon trip to Maui, HI, including round-trip air transportation provided by Maui Visitors Bureau from Los Angeles International Airport (winner is responsible for transportation to and from Los Angeles International Airport) and a Harlequin Romance Package, including hotel accomodations (double occupancy) at the Hyatt Regency Maui Resort and Spa, dinner for (2) two at Swan Court, a sunset sail on Kiele V and a spa treatment for the winner (approximate retail value: $4,000); (5) Five runner-up prizes of a $1000 gift certificate to selected retail outlets to be determined by Sponsor (retail value $1000 ea.). Prizes consist of only those items listed as part of the prize. Limit one prize per person. All prizes are valued in U.S. currency.

8. For a list of winners (available after December 17, 2001) send a self-addressed, stamped envelope to: Harlequin Walk Down the Aisle Contest 1197 Winners, P.O. Box 4200 Blair, NE 68009-4200 or you may access the www.eHarlequin.com Web site through January 15, 2002.

Contest sponsored by Torstar Corp., P.O. Box 9042, Buffalo, NY 14269-9042, U.S.A.

PHWDACONT2